MANNHEIM STEAMROLLER

Christmas

A Night Like No Other

Story by Chip Davis
Written by Jill Stern

P O C K E T   B O O K S
New York London Toronto Sydney Singapore

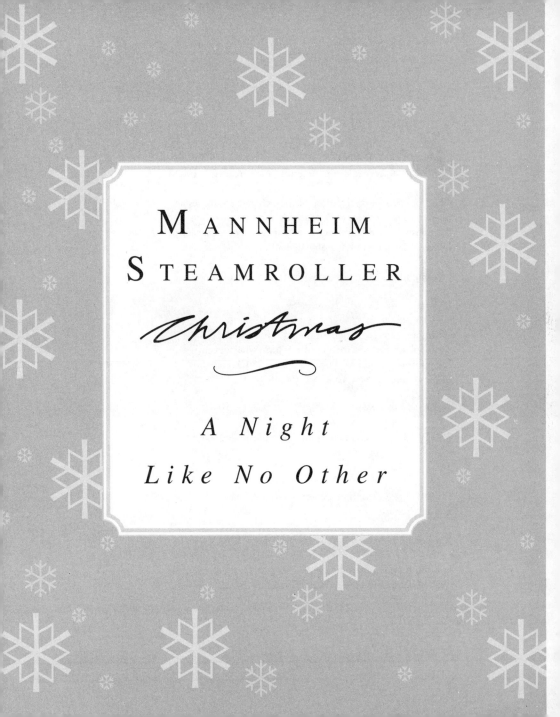

M ANNHEIM S TEAMROLLER

Christmas

A Night Like No Other

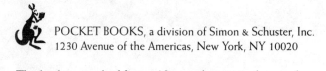

POCKET BOOKS, a division of Simon & Schuster, Inc.
1230 Avenue of the Americas, New York, NY 10020

Illustrations by David J. Negron, Sr.

ISBN: 0-7434-8088-0

First Pocket Books hardcover edition November 2003

10 9 8 7 6 5 4 3 2 1

Manufactured in the United States of America

For information regarding special discounts for bulk purchases, please contact Simon & Schuster Special Sales at 1-800-456-6798 or business@simonandschuster.com

To my family
Evan, Elyse, Kelly
Trisha

Thanks to Chip Davis for the story, Liate Stehlik for the opportunity, and Micki Nuding for the enthusiastic encouragement. And special thanks to Dave, Maddy, and Caleb, whose patience and support make our particular family tradition of "mommy working late at the office" possible.

—JPS

Prologue

YOU NEVER KNOW *how old you're going to be when you learn the most important lesson of your life. I was ten. That Christmas, I had a once-in-a-lifetime adventure—the kind you know you'll want to tell your kids about someday. But when I had kids, I figured they'd never believe me if*

I told them. And so I never did. Until one Christmas Eve, nearly thirty years later, when I realized that if I didn't share the lesson I had learned, they might never believe in anything. . . .

"EVERYBODY READY *to go get the tree?*"

I stood in the doorway, stamping my feet and shaking snowflakes out of my hair. Melting snow dripped off my overcoat and puddled on the flag-stone floor of the entryway.

My nine-year-old son, Daniel, stared in disbelief. "I'm not going out in that blizzard," he said, gesturing toward the bay windows that flanked our front door.

"Me, either." His five-year-old sister Lily appeared behind him, clutching the camel from the Christmas crèche in one hand and one of the Three Kings in the other. "I'm playing zoo with the Christmas dolls."

I sighed. Christmas Eve, and the worst storm in thirty years was expected to blanket the Midwest. I looked out at the driving white flakes again.

"C'mon, kids," I insisted. "It's a family tradition. We always get the tree on Christmas Eve. We need to put it up tonight so it's ready when Santa comes."

Daniel rolled his eyes at the mention of Santa. Even Lily looked dubious.

"You go get it, Daddy," Lily said.

"Yeah, you're the one who always wants to go get the tree on the same day, at the same place," Daniel added. "You get all crazy at Christmastime."

"What do you mean, crazy?" I asked.

"You know, always having to decorate the same way, eat the same stuff, play the same music. You're in a rut, Dad," Daniel explained.

"It's called tradition," I said, louder than I meant to.

My wife, Jen, appeared in the doorway, wiping floury hands on her jeans.

"It is snowing awfully hard, hon," she said. "Are you sure you want to go out in the woods in this weather?"

I shot her a look. She should know better.

"Hey, Dad, there's this great site online, www.xmastrees4U, where you can order up a tree and they deliver it right to the door." Sam—at thirteen, the resident computer expert in the household—ventured out of his room at the top of the stairs to add his opinion. "They deliver in twenty-four hours, up until 9:00 A.M. on Christmas Day. You can even order a predecorated tree. That would save us a lot of work," he added helpfully.

"We're not ordering a tree online," I sputtered. "And we're not waiting to see if the weather lifts, and I'm not going out alone."

My family stood and stared at me.

"We are going to go get a tree, and we are going NOW," I roared.

AS I WATCHED my family sullenly struggling into their parkas and snow boots, I'll admit I gave some thought to Sam's online Christmas tree store. Just a click of the mouse, and the finest tree money could buy would show up at our door. Was this really how the kids thought we should prepare for Christmas? Just go about our normal routines in December and then on the twenty-fourth simply surf the Net and have Christmas arrive via UPS?

How could they think like this? Didn't they know how important each of the traditions I treasured was to me? To our family? There was only one way to find out.

I stood between my family and the door. "Don't you guys like going out together to get the tree?" I asked.

Sam shook his head. A flat 'no.'

Daniel shrugged his shoulders.

"It's always such a long walk," Lily said.

My wife stared at her feet.

"What about all of the rest of this stuff?" I made a sweeping gesture toward our beautifully decorated living room. "What about hanging the stockings together? Or listening to Christmas carols while we decorate the tree? Or decorating the house with holly and mistletoe and evergreen garlands? Or setting up the crèche? Or Santa? Or gifts?"

"Whoa, Dad. Don't go overboard," Sam said. "We totally care about the gifts."

Daniel and Lily nodded in support.

"But the rest of the traditions of the holiday?" I said. "You wouldn't miss them?"

"Nothing says Christmas like new software," Sam said.

"Santa could just leave my stuff on the couch," Lily said helpfully.

"And you and Mom would have more time to shop for us if you didn't have to do all this other stuff for Christmas," Daniel added.

My heart sank. How had this happened? I had thought that by sharing the holiday traditions with my kids, they would appreciate how important each one was. They'd know that Christmas was about so much more than brightly wrapped presents.

But I now realized that I'd never actually told my children why the traditions were so important to me. Why they were so important to all of us. For all these years, instead of truly embracing Christmas, my family had been merely going through the motions. And no one knew better than I did that Christmas was about much more than just going through the motions.

I had to do something. And fast.

"All right, winter gear off," I commanded.

Surprised and delighted by the sudden change in plan, the kids stripped off their layers of outdoor clothes.

"Family meeting in the living room," I announced.

Looks of relief turned to looks of dismay as the kids marched single file into the living room.

"I think I may have left the oven on." My wife beat a hasty retreat to the kitchen.

I sat down in an overstuffed armchair and studied my children, who were perched across from me in a row on the couch.

"I know exactly how you feel," I said.

Lily nodded earnestly as if to say, "Of course you do, Daddy." For a tiny moment I allowed myself to bask in the omnipotence bestowed on parents by their youngest children.

A quick glance at Sam dispelled any notion of parental sway. He was rolling his eyes with the pained expression particular to teenagers required to spend time in serious conversation with a well-intentioned adult.

Finally I focused on Daniel. He was staring at me with the very special look nine-year-old boys reserve for their fathers. The look that says, "How could you possibly know what it's like to be a kid at Christmas?"

A lecture on the importance of Christmas traditions wasn't going to work, I realized. And then I knew what I had to do.

"I'm going to tell you guys a story," I began. "Think of it as a new tradition; the kind of story you can tell your kids each Christmas."

Sam groaned audibly as he moved down to sprawl on the floor.

"A story from a book? Or a made-up story?" Lily was already interested. She came over to climb into the chair next to me.

"A story I know by heart," I answered. I'd just update some of the details so they'd relate to it better.

I glanced out the window at the falling snow as it swirled past, erasing the landscape outside. As the storm outside picked up strength, I took a deep breath and began the story I had waited too long to share.

"It was a day very much like today, in a town very much like this town. When a boy who didn't think Christmas was worth all the fuss embarked on an adventure that changed the way he thought about Christmas forever. . . .

One

EVAN DARLING TRUDGED home from school, kicking at snow banks and grumbling. Only 4:30, and the afternoon sky was already dark. It had been snowing all week and the toboggan run at the end of his street was perfectly packed. But there was no way his mother would let him go out sledding

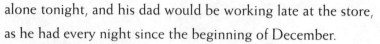

alone tonight, and his dad would be working late at the store, as he had every night since the beginning of December.

Cold water seeped in over the top of his boot as he tried, but failed, to clear a huge slush puddle near the curb. Evan longed for spring. He imagined the big green field behind his house, freshly mowed—perfect for an after-dinner baseball game. He thought about how his dad always made sure to leave work early so they could play a game of catch before dinner. Stopping in the middle of the sidewalk, Evan closed his eyes, letting the thick snowflakes melt on his lids. He pictured sunshine, white fluffy clouds, new green leaves against a bright blue sky. He opened his eyes. Bare tree branches stood in black silhouette against the overcast sky and piles of snow—turned gray and sooty by traffic—slopped up and over the curbs. Evan sighed, feeling as though spring might never come again.

With cold water squishing in his boot at each step, Evan turned onto Main Street. The little shops lining both sides of the street were bustling with people rushing in and out, their arms full of bags and packages. Dark-green pine garland twisted around the poles of the streetlights, which were just beginning to flicker on. Small white lights framed the windows of some shops, while bright red and green flashing lights bordered the doorways of others. Cars moved slowly down the street, carefully navigating around the many shoppers crossing the road.

Above the street, stars outlined in tiny white lights hung on cables stretched from one side to the other. Main Street glowed with Christmas spirit, as if to cancel out the advancing darkness of the winter afternoon. But Evan's mood was as gloomy as the snow clouds piling up in the late afternoon sky, and the blazing lights and cheerful decorations did nothing to lift his spirits.

In fact, as far as Evan was concerned, the whole Christmas thing was completely out of control.

Take the annual Holidayle Elementary School Christmas pageant, for instance. Evan's class had had to stay late to work on their number. Even though the performance for the whole school was tomorrow, half the class still couldn't remember their lines, and the other half only wanted to talk about all the presents they were expecting to get on Christmas, which was just three days away.

Evan had made the mistake of saying that he'd hoped Santa would bring him a new CD player for his room, and a couple of the sixth graders had overheard. They had teased him mercilessly before hurling him into the snow banks outside of school. Not because of the CD player, but for saying he'd hoped Santa would bring it. Evan finally said he just pretended to believe because of his little sister, but even as he said it, it felt like a betrayal. The idea of Santa—who Evan pictured as taller and thinner, kind of like Professor Dumbledore from Harry Potter, only in long red robes—was one of the few things Evan thought was really special about Christmas. Santa—and Christmas carols.

Evan loved Christmas carols. Listening to songs like "Silent Night" or "White Christmas" gave him a warm feeling that started in his chest and spread through his whole body. He knew all the words to all the songs that had to do with Christmas, and he loved to sing them. To Evan, they were like magical incantations that conjured up the very season.

Sure, some of them made no sense at all, like "Here We Come a'Wassailing." He thought that maybe wassailing was some winter sport, like parasailing, only in the snow. But it didn't really matter what it was about—he still loved the song.

Evan began to hum as he walked down the street. By the time he'd worked his way through "Joy to the World," he was feeling a little better. At the end of Main Street, Evan saw another Christmas sight that made him smile. He broke into a jog and crossed over to the parking lot next to the local pharmacy and market.

The parking lot was empty of cars. At the far end, an old camper with a flat trailer attached to the back was pulled up next to the building. A little distance from the trailer, a metal barrel that had been sawed in half held a small wood fire. Two large logs sat on either side to serve as chairs. From the middle of the lot to the sidewalk, rows and rows of fresh-cut fir trees leaned against sawhorses. Evan walked between the rows of trees, admiring how the fresh snow tipped their branches. The tall trees screened out the bustle and noise of the streets beyond, and Evan imagined he was deep in a forest.

"Merry Christmas, Evan."

Evan jumped at the sound of the voice, even though he expected it.

"Hey, Leon." Evan turned around and smiled. "Merry Christmas to you."

Leon Tannenbaum was the most unusual-looking grown-up Evan had ever seen. He was thin and small, not much taller than Evan, and had shocking red hair that stuck out in random tufts from under his tattered winter hat. He had twinkling blue eyes that all but disappeared in a web of wrinkles and creases when he smiled, which was almost constantly. He wore many layers of brightly colored winter clothes, not seeming to mind that the bright green stripes on his pants competed for attention with the bold red and white diamonds on his sweater. He completed his costume with several gaily striped scarves wrapped around his neck and gloves with the fingers cut off.

Every year since Evan could remember, Leon Tannenbaum and his trailer of fresh-cut trees had pulled into Holidayle a few days before Christmas and set up shop in the parking lot. Evan's family had never bought a tree from Leon. Instead, Evan's dad always insisted on following the family tradition of marching out into the woods behind their house, cutting down a fresh tree, and dragging it home. Still, Evan looked forward to seeing Leon every year, and Leon never seemed to mind that Evan wasn't a customer—he always seemed genuinely glad to see him.

"Got a new CD to lure the customers in," Leon said, grinning widely. He knew Evan loved music and they often compared notes on their favorite versions of Christmas songs. Leon ran over to the large boom box that sat on a makeshift table near the sidewalk, twisted the volume to high, and stood expectantly, his head cocked to one side as a lush melody filled the air.

"It's a medieval carol," he said, waving a hand in the air in time to the music.

Evan had never heard anything like it. He listened and heard strings and bells and maybe a flute. When the singers came on, Evan couldn't understand the language they were singing in, but it didn't matter. He closed his eyes and let the music swirl around him. Breathing deeply, he smelled pine trees and wood smoke and fresh snow.

"It's what Christmas is all about, isn't it?" Leon said softly.

Evan opened his eyes and nodded. "It's perfect," he agreed. "But I can't understand what they're singing."

"It's in Latin," Leon explained. "An ancient language for an ancient holiday."

Evan tried to picture an ancient Christmas—a celebration in a time before electric tree lights and shopping malls. Frankly, he couldn't imagine what people ever did.

"Have you got time for a cup of hot cocoa?" Leon motioned toward a thermos sitting next to the boom box.

"Not today," Evan said. "I'm already late. My mom probably

has about a million things for me to do—just 'cuz it's Christmas. You know how it is."

"I'll take a snow check then," Leon said, waving good-bye.

E VAN J O G G E D down the street. He could get home a lot
quicker if he cut through the woods behind the parking lot—
his house was right on the other side. But it was already dark,
and the woods were hard enough to navigate in the snow in
daylight. Sticking to the main roads, he soon arrived home.

The white colonial house sat on the last lot at the end of a
dead-end street. There was no missing it; Evan's mom had
gone nuts decorating for the holiday. Huge evergreen wreaths
swathed in red ribbon hung from the upstairs windows, illuminated by floodlights set into the lawn. Another enormous
wreath decorated the front door. Electric candles glowed in all
the windows facing the street. The lamppost at the edge of the
lawn was wrapped in red-and-white to look like a candy cane,
and wire sculptures of reindeer, wrapped in little white lights,
were posed along the path leading up to the house.

Going around the side, Evan let himself in the back door

and dropped his backpack on the kitchen floor with a thud. His mother stood at the open door to the oven, shoveling trays of cookies onto the wire racks. She didn't even turn around. His younger sister, Elyse, was sitting at the kitchen table frosting gingerbread men as if they were on an assembly line: swipe the frosting, stick on two raisins for eyes, three cinnamon dots for buttons, move to another tray. She never looked up from the rows of cookies, lined up like soldiers at attention.

Evan pulled off his knit cap and scratched his head until his brown hair stood up in spikes on the top of his head. He hated the itchy wool hat with its snowflake pattern and matching mittens, but his grandma sent him an identical set every year for Christmas. Dropping the hat and mittens on a chair next to the door, he shrugged out of his parka. He inhaled deeply. The spicy smell of gingerbread filled his nostrils. Okay, so maybe there was something else to appreciate about the Christmas season—his mom never baked like this at any other time of year. He walked over to the island in the center of the kitchen and broke the leg off a cooling gingerbread man.

"Mooooom! He's eating the gingerbread men!" Elyse

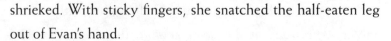

shrieked. With sticky fingers, she snatched the half-eaten leg out of Evan's hand.

"Evan James Darling!" His mother nearly dropped the tray of cookies she was putting into the oven. "Those are for the second-grade party tomorrow!"

"Sorry," Evan mumbled, crumbs spraying out of his mouth.

"You're about to be very sorry, young man," his mother snapped, staring pointedly at the puddles of melted snow that dotted the kitchen floor and pooled around Evan's boots. She pushed her light brown bangs back, leaving a trail of flour across her forehead. She was wearing an apron that was decorated with Christmas trees and teddy bears, but she didn't look very festive. She looked hot and tired.

Behind her mother's back, Elyse stuck her tongue out at Evan and went back to decorating.

"Sorry," Evan said again, trying to slip out of his boots without dripping any more water on the floor.

Evan's older sister, Kelly, came to the door of the kitchen, pointed to her mother, and held her finger to her lips.

"Be quiet," she mouthed.

Kelly was already dressed in her parka and was carrying her boots. As she began to tiptoe toward the back door, Evan and

Elyse watched her silently cross behind their mother's back. Kelly put her hand on the doorknob and began to open the door slowly.

"Where are you going, young lady?" Evan's mother didn't even turn around. She just bent down and put another tray of gingerbread into the oven.

"To the mall. I need to get a present for Mitch."

Mitch was Kelly's boyfriend, and as far as Evan could tell, the only thing she cared about besides how her hair looked.

"I thought you got Mitch a sweater."

"He can't use a sweater in Mexico," Kelly said. "I thought I'd try to find him a snorkel at the sports shop. It's not too late for me to look for a new bathing suit, either."

Evan began inching out of the room. He knew what was coming. Kelly had been begging their parents to allow her to go away with Mitch and his family. They were leaving on Christmas Eve day and wouldn't be home until two days after Christmas. Mitch's family went on a different vacation every year at Christmastime. Evan had overheard Mitch's dad saying that Christmas was just a long weekend off from work, and they might as well take advantage of it and go somewhere really great. Mitch told Evan that they had gone to Mexico once be-

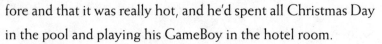

fore and that it was really hot, and he'd spent all Christmas Day in the pool and playing his GameBoy in the hotel room.

Kelly had been pestering their parents about this trip since the beginning of December.

"What's wrong with wanting to do something different for Christmas for a change? Why do we always have to do the same things?"

"We've discussed this over and over again, Kelly. You're not going away over Christmas. It's a time to be with family." Evan's mother always started out calmly.

"And friends. And loved ones," Kelly pointed out.

"And *family.*" Evan's mother turned around to face Kelly.

Please, Evan thought, *don't roll your eyes.*

Kelly rolled her eyes.

"You've been to the mall every day for the last two weeks. I could use a little help here," his mother continued.

Don't say "whatever," Evan silently pleaded.

"Whatever," Kelly said sullenly.

Evan winced.

"That's it. Take off that coat," Evan's mother's voice rose. "You're going to stay right here tonight and help us finish up some Christmas chores."

Kelly shrugged out of her coat and slumped into a kitchen chair. She began eating the raisins that Elyse was using for eyes.

Christmas chores, thought Evan. That's all this dumb holiday is good for. A bunch of things that you're supposed to *want* to do just because they're called *traditions*: chop down trees, bring 'em inside, string them with lights, make eggnog, shop all the time until you've bought tons of stuff that no one wants—like socks and underwear—-drag in holly and pine garland, decorate the house.

Evan frowned as he remembered the worst Christmas tradition of all: the ball of mistletoe.

Last year Amanda Rose, who lived across the street, had planted a big kiss right on Evan's lips. Evan had stood there frozen—turning as red as the velvet ribbon decorating the banister in the hallway, where she had trapped him—as all the adults laughed. He shuddered and rubbed the back of his hand across his mouth.

Traditions, phooey. What's the point of them anyway? Why not just celebrate Christmas in a new way every year? Maybe Mitch's family is on to something.

Two

EVAN YAWNED and rubbed his eyes. He swirled his Cinnamon Christmas Puffs cereal idly around in the bowl, scooping the little red and green nuggets onto his spoon and then dropping them back into the milk. He was exhausted. Last night's Christmas chore had been the family signing of the annual Christmas photo card. They'd had to wait until his dad came home from the store—late as usual—then his mother had made everyone sit at the dining room table and passed the cards around for their signatures. Evan's fingers had cramped as he scrawled his name on card after card. He had grown so bored staring at the smiling faces of his family—all dressed in matching red-and-green sweaters—that he had drawn a little mustache on his sister Kelly's picture on a couple of the cards. Just a little one. Really. Barely a line.

Unfortunately, Kelly couldn't take a joke. Well, one thing led to another and she ripped up the cards. And that set their dad off, hollering about how he had calculated exactly how many cards they needed to send out this year, which somehow turned into a speech about how they should all be extra good to each other at this time of year. By the time he wound down, Kelly had stomped upstairs in a huff, Evan had been sent to his room for punishment, and Elyse—who nobody had noticed had fallen asleep at the end of the table—got carried up to her bed.

When Evan had crept downstairs later to apologize, he found his mom and dad still sitting at the table, scribbling away, piles of finished cards stacked sloppily in front of them.

Feliz Navidad. She was really rubbing it in about Mexico. Evan braced himself for the inevitable explosion, but his mother had already turned back to the counter and was packing up the gingerbread men in orderly rows.

Grabbing his mittens and hat, Evan shrugged into his backpack and trotted out to wait at the curb for the bus. He really wasn't looking forward to the pageant. Mr. Shariff, his fifth-grade teacher, had written a play about the traditions of Christmas, but he had made them "hip," he proudly told the class.

Evan's number was a rap song called "Yo, Little Town of Bethlehem."

"HEY, EVAN, got your costume for the play?" Evan's best friend, Maddy, waved him over to the empty seat next to her on the bus.

His costume! Evan unzipped his backpack in a panic, shoving aside crumpled art papers and an old comic book. He saw a hint of blue at the bottom of the pack.

And now it was morning—the morning of the fifth Christmas pageant. Another day wasted at school. A day when Evan would have no chance to get out to play new snow that was drifting past the kitchen window in ery flakes.

"Don't forget to come straight home after school Evan." His mother whisked his nearly empty bowl out fro der his spoon. "Your father is coming home early so we c cut the tree down. We'll put it up tomorrow, on Christmas

"Why aren't we getting the tree on Christmas Eve *always* get the tree on Christmas Eve!" Evan said.

"They're forecasting the blizzard of the century to tonight," his mother told him. "We'll probably be compl snowed in by tomorrow afternoon, so we have to make we get everything done."

She smacked her hand to her forehead. "That reminds need to pick up some things at the mall this afternoon. I'll Elyse with me, but I won't be able to pick you up after Christmas pageant. You'll have to walk home."

She fixed Evan with a steady gaze. "Straight home."

Evan nodded glumly.

Kelly wandered into the kitchen, wearing a T-shirt that

"Got it," he said in relief, pulling the crumpled shepherd's robe to the top.

"Geez, Ev, that's kind of a mess," Maddy said, frowning.

"I don't see why we have to wear a stupid dress, anyway." The costume was just another thing Evan hated about the pageant.

"Technically, it's a robe," Maddy pointed out.

Evan shoved the blue *robe* back into his backpack. "I'll be the shepherd who didn't have time to take his stuff to the dry cleaner," he said. "I'll be the shepherd who was so busy doing chores to get ready for Christmas that he totally *missed* the whole holiday." He was on a roll.

"You're really turning into a Scrooge, you know?" Maddy said.

"I just don't see the point of all these 'traditions' we have to follow. I mean, why is it so important to have a tree decorated with lights? Why does everything have to be all red and green? Is there *really* a Santa Claus? And if there is, what's his deal, and if there isn't, then why does everyone keep talking about him?" Evan took a deep breath. "And what the heck is wassailing anyway?"

"So what's your point? That we should skip all the Christ-

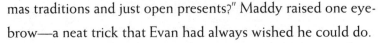

mas traditions and just open presents?" Maddy raised one eye-brow—a neat trick that Evan had always wished he could do.

"Yeah, that would suit me just fine," he replied, knowing that wasn't what he wanted at all. Evan was a reasonable guy, and if there was a reason for doing something, then he just wanted to know what it was.

The bus pulled up to Holidayle Elementary.

"Well, c'mon, Scrooge." Maddy grinned, tossing her long brown braids over her shoulders. "You know what they say: It's not Christmas until the shepherds reach Bethlehem."

Evan followed Maddy into their classroom where Mr. Shar-iff, a small, wiry, balding man, was dashing about madly.

"Okay, Shepherds, over here. Camels, take your places! Wise Men? Wise Men! Let's get moving."

Evan moved over to take his place next to Jack Nelson and Caleb Stern, the two other shepherds. He sighed as Jack elbowed him in the ribs as he moved into position. Caleb and Jack were always goofing around—changing the words to the song, messing up the dance moves, trying to get each other—or, even better, Evan—in trouble with Mr. Shariff.

"All right, let's take it from the top!" Mr. Shariff stepped back among the rows of desks, his arms cocked on his hips.

Evan, Jack, and Caleb stepped forward. Pointing their fingers down, as if at a little village below them, they rapped:

> *Yo, little town of Bethlehem*
> *Sure got some sleepy eyes*
> *Above the huts where you're sacked out*
> *No word from the stars in the skies*

"Woohoo!" Mr. Shariff pumped his fist in the air when they
finished. "Kids, that was great. You really rocked."

The three shepherds shuffled back to their original posi-
tions in the tableau.

"Hang on," Mr. Shariff said—and Evan could practically see
the light bulb pop up over his head. Mr. Shariff was famous for
his last minute, so-called-brilliant ideas.

"We need a big finish to this number. Evan, you stand here,
like this." He moved Evan slightly downstage, and had him raise
his hand as if to point to the Christmas Star. He positioned Jack
and Caleb right behind him and had them get down on one
knee and gesture dramatically in the same direction.

Evan was pretty nervous with Jack and Caleb out of his sight,
but Mr. Shariff was having an artistic vision, so the scene was set.

"Okay, then Jack and Caleb get up, then Evan leads every-one off to stage right." Mr. Shariff grinned happily. "This is gonna be great!"

NOT MUCH ELSE got done that day in Evan's class-room. Not much ever did right before the Christmas holidays. Somebody's mom brought in gingerbread men and someone else's dad sent in candy canes. Jack and Caleb treated the class to a loud rendition of "Jingle Bells, Batman Smells," and Mrs. Hunter, the librarian, came down to the classroom to read "The Night Before Christmas."

Finally, Evan found himself standing backstage among elves, dancing candy canes, a choir of angels, and a farmyard's worth of nativity animals. The rest of the school sat out in the darkened auditorium. He could hear the shuffling of feet and the excited hum of voices.

Evan was nervous. Last night he'd had the nightmare com-mon to many performers: the one where you get onstage and realize that you're in your underwear. His dad had told him not to worry, that instead he should picture the audience all dressed in their underwear. Evan thought of Mrs. Hanover, the cafeteria lady, and shuddered. No way was he going to try that technique.

"Evan!" Evan jumped as Mr. Shariff snuck up behind him and hissed in his ear. "I can see your jeans. Shepherds did not wear jeans."

Evan was pretty sure shepherds never did a rap version of "O Little Town of Bethlehem," either. He looked over at Jack and Caleb, hoping against hope for some solidarity. Grinning evilly, Jack and Caleb hiked up their long robes to expose gym shorts.

Foiled again. Evan sighed and slid out of his jeans. A cool draft blew up against his legs. Great—now he really felt like he was wearing a dress. Mr. Shariff was gesturing for the Shepherds to take the stage, so Evan gave one last tug to the long zipper that ran from the neck of his robe to the hem just above his sandals. And then he was marching across the stage, followed by Jack and Caleb, who mercifully didn't change the words to the song, just bellowed them out like they were contestants for a spot on MTV Raps or something.

The audience burst into applause when they finished and Evan allowed himself a small smile. Behind him, Jack and Caleb stood up from their pose. "Get moving, Evan," Jack hissed.

The audience had stopped applauding and sat waiting politely. Evan stepped forward quickly. As he did, he felt his costume snag. Mr. Shariff was frantically waving to the Shepherds to get offstage. Flustered, Evan yanked at the back of his robe and lurched forward again. He heard some snickers behind him, then some outbreaks of laughter from the audience. He had to get off the stage! As he took a giant step forward, he glanced back over his shoulder. To his horror, he realized that Jack and Caleb were standing firmly on the hem of his costume, and had no intention of moving. But it was too late to stop walking forward. Evan heard the roar of laughter from the auditorium as he felt the zipper give way. With as much dignity as he could muster, Evan walked right out of his shepherd's robe and right offstage. Then he slid back into his jeans and slipped out of the auditorium.

Picture them in *their* underwear, indeed.

THE SNOW WAS falling steadily as Evan made his way home. Icy flakes clung to his eyelashes and stung his cheeks.

Shrugging deeper into his parka, he leaned into the wind, walking home on autopilot.

"Hey, Evan, why so glum, chum?" Leon was sitting outside his camper, warming his hands at the fire. He waved Evan over.

Evan shuffled over. He sat down on a milk crate across from Leon and leaned in close to the warm embers.

"I hate Christmas," he said flatly.

"You can't mean that!" Leon looked shocked.

"Well, I don't hate Christmas itself," Evan reassured him. "I hate signing cards, and mistletoe, and tromping through the snow to chop down a tree, and I *especially* hate Christmas pageants. All the stuff everybody says we have to do to make it seem like Christmas."

"All that 'stuff' is exactly what makes the season special," Leon said. "People have done those things for centuries."

"Then why does everybody want to make it modern?" Evan asked. "Like changing Christmas Carols to rap songs. Everyone seems to think that stuff is so cool."

"Traditions can change and evolve over time," Leon said thoughtfully. "But the ones that last—the ones passed down

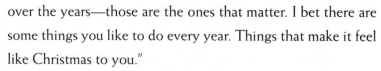

over the years—those are the ones that matter. I bet there are some things you like to do every year. Things that make it feel like Christmas to you."

Evan nodded. "I like the music," he admitted. "And lying underneath the Christmas tree in the dark, so all the lights sparkle overhead like stars. And the smell of gingerbread."

"Exactly." Leon stared at Evan thoughtfully. "Hang on, buddy. I've got something I want to show you."

Evan watched as Leon jumped up and pulled open the creaky door to the camper. The little man disappeared inside and Evan heard mysterious bumps and thumps. After a few minutes Leon emerged, holding a box triumphantly overhead.

"Found it," he declared.

Sitting back down on his bench, he began to push aside masses of red and green tissue paper.

"Close your eyes and put out your hands," he told Evan. "No peeking."

Evan squinched his eyes tightly shut, his palms obediently held upward.

He felt a weight rest in them.

"Okay," Leon said. "Open!"

Evan opened his eyes and stared. In his hands he held the

most beautiful snow globe he had ever seen. He ran his palm lightly over the smooth glass dome. Inside, a perfect Christmas village sat at the foot of a great castle. He turned the globe upside down, and then righted it again. As the sparkling snow swirled down, he admired the tiny evergreen trees and the cozy white houses nestled among them. The scene looked so real, he swore he could see smoke coming from the chimneys and drifting past the red roofs.

He pictured the families inside the tiny homes, gathered around fragrant Christmas trees shimmering with tiny white lights. He could smell the roasting chestnuts and hear the angelic voices of a choir singing "Silent Night."

The huge castle glowed golden above the village, with colorful banners draped from its ramparts. Evan knew the halls were ablaze with torchlight, and lords and ladies in their finest clothes were gliding down halls draped with ivy and evergreen. He pressed his nose close to the glass globe.

When he glanced up, Leon was watching him.

"See the train on the outside of the snow globe?" Leon asked.

Evan nodded.

"Turn it."

Evan gently took hold of the train's smokestack and wound it backward. When he let go, the train began to travel around the snow globe as the sweet sound of a music box filled the air. Though he thought he knew every Christmas song there was, Evan could not identify the tune. But he knew instinctively that it was a Christmas carol.

He held the snow globe up against the winter sky, watching the flakes gently drift down.

"It's like holding Christmas in my hands," he whispered.

Leon looked satisfied. "I knew you were the right person."

Evan held out the snow globe. "Thanks for letting me see it," he said, reluctant to give it back.

"It's yours," Leon said. "Consider it an early Christmas gift."

"Really?" Evan hugged his treasure close, as if Leon might change his mind. "Thanks! I'll take really good care of it."

"I know you will," Leon said.

Suddenly Evan realized that the sky had grown even darker. How long had he been sitting in front of the fire?

"Hey, Leon, do you know what time it is?"

"Sorry, Evan, I never wear a watch." Leon glanced up at the darkening sky. "Looks like the storm's about to pick up, though."

"My mom is gonna kill me." Evan stood. "We're supposed to go out and chop down a Christmas tree."

He looked around at all the trees Leon had left. "Not that there's anything wrong with your trees," he said quickly. "It's just some stupid tradition of my dad's."

"No tradition worth keeping is stupid," Leon told him gently. "You'd better hurry home."

Evan reached into his backpack and pulled out his tattered shepherd's robe. He carefully wrapped it around the snow globe and gently placed the bundle in his backpack. Slipping his arms through the shoulder straps, he then waved good-bye to his friend and started off across the parking lot at a steady jog.

At the edge of the parking lot, Evan hesitated. The snow was swirling in a thick curtain of white. Squinting against the storm, he glanced across the street. He could barely see to the other curb. He could hear his mother's voice in his head: "Evan James Darling, didn't I tell you to be home right after school? Where have you been?"

Hoping to make up for lost time, Evan abruptly changed direction, ducking into the woods between the parking lot and his house. He reasoned that the snow wouldn't be falling so thickly in the woods and he'd be able to get home faster.

About halfway through the woods, Evan realized that his reasoning had been flawed. Seriously flawed.

The snow was sweeping through the woods in blinding sheets. The hard-packed paths that marked the favorite sledding spots running down into the ravine were hidden under the shifting snowdrifts. Evan struggled to make his way through the deepest part of the snow, once getting stuck nearly up to his thighs, and another time having his boot sucked right off his foot.

He was growing colder and more exhausted by the minute. He glanced around frantically, looking for the welcoming lights of his house twinkling through the trees. He stood still, straining his ears to detect sounds of traffic, or any other noises indicating in which direction the street lay. The silence roared in his ears.

Don't panic, he told himself. He turned slowly in a circle, noting that his footsteps had already been erased by the swirling storm.

His nose had begun a steady drip and his eyes were tearing from the wind. Evan struggled forward.

"Help!" he shouted as loud as he could. The biting winds

snatched his words and whisked them off among the bare branches. "Help!" His voice was pleading now.

Evan's legs felt like lead, but he willed them to move faster and faster until he was running and stumbling though the drifts. A dry tree branch snagged his cap, but Evan didn't dare stop. He had to go forward. He knew that now it was him against the storm. He was in a life-and-death battle, only yards away from his house.

He staggered into a deep patch of snow and lost his balance. Evan threw his arms out to break his fall, but he still sank elbow-deep into the drifts. Righting himself, he continued his desperate struggle forward. He no longer knew if he was headed toward home; he just knew he had to get out of the woods. There were people and warm stores and his own house on either side of him. As long as he wasn't going in circles, he'd be all right.

Don't panic, he told himself again.

But the tears in his eyes weren't from the cold anymore.

His world was starkly black-and-white—the night and the drifting, falling snow.

Evan staggered another step forward, and suddenly he was

falling, tumbling end over end like a human avalanche. *I guess I've found the ravine,* he managed to think, as his backpack fell loose from his flailing arms.

And suddenly the ground rose up to meet him with stunning force. *I didn't know snow could be so hard,* Evan thought. A sharp pain shot through his head—and his whole world faded into darkness.

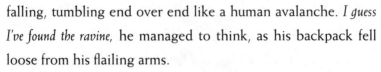

J E N S W U N G T H R O U G H *the door to the living room, carrying a tray of sandwiches and steaming mugs of cinnamon hot chocolate. "Lunchtime," she announced. "Actually, it's nearly two o'clock."*

"No wonder I'm starving," Sam exclaimed, shoving half a sandwich into his mouth.

"The storm's really picking up," Jen said. "I've been listening to the news station on the radio and they're forecasting up to four feet by morning."

Outside, I could hear the wind howling as it blew past the corners of the house. Sheets of snow battered the windows. The afternoon light was dim and the living room was shadowed in gray. I reached up to turn on the reading lamp next to my chair. A warm glow filled the living room. And then the light blinked once, twice, and then off.

"Uh-oh, there goes the power," Jen said, getting up to peer out the window.

"They're not likely to get a crew out in this storm," I said. "Might as well settle in."

Jen went to the dining room and came back with several tall candles. As she set them around the room, I kindled a small fire in the fireplace. The kids ate their lunch contentedly, watching us work.

With the fire glowing and the candles at the ready, the room was a cozy refuge from the storm. Jen left again and returned from the kitchen with a plate of warm gingerbread.

"I made it for any carolers who might come by," she explained, "but I'm sure we won't have any tonight."

She was right. It was looking like we'd all be snowbound by nightfall. I thought about the perfect Christmas tree—waiting for us in the woods behind the house.

"Finish the story, Daddy," Lily tugged at my arm.

"Yeah, what happens to Evan?" Daniel wanted to know.

I picked up a mug of hot chocolate. I had them right where I wanted them. The weather forecasters were always overly pessimistic. I was betting the storm would ease up, and we could cut down a tree later.

Worst case, I'd go out and buy a tree—just this once.

Three

EVAN SAT UP slowly, gingerly rubbing his head. Thick white snowflakes drifted lazily down. The the storm had slowed, he realized. He stood up slowly and prepared to hike up the other side of the ravine. With relief, he realized that he could see the outlines of the streets and buildings again.

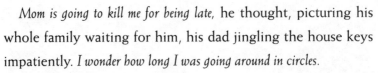

Mom is going to kill me for being late, he thought, picturing his whole family waiting for him, his dad jingling the house keys impatiently. *I wonder how long I was going around in circles.*

Evan walked to the edge of the tree line and stopped dead. He took off his mitten and rubbed his hand across his eyes. He was on a sidewalk, true. But it wasn't a sidewalk in Holidayle. Frantically, Evan spun around again, looking for the strings of blinking red-and-green lights that illuminated the Main Street stores. But all he saw were small, neat shops—shuttered and dark. There were no signs of life. No shoppers bustled up and down the streets, no storefronts blazed with neon and twinkling lights. No Christmas carols blared from tinny loudspeakers. All was quiet. Too quiet.

Evan began to run down the sidewalk. Surely he'd find someone who could tell him where he was. He turned down a side street and slowed to a walk. He was in a neighborhood of neat cottages, but, like the stores, they appeared to be completely deserted. There were no cars parked in the driveways, no sleds strewn across the lawns. The houses, too, were completely dark.

Evan slumped against a snowbank, stunned. He had no idea where he was, but wherever it was, it was a ghost town. He tipped his head back against the cold snow, his thoughts whirling. He stared up into the sky—a strangely shiny, dark, moonless sky.

In the distance, Evan thought he saw a flicker of light. He climbed up onto the snowbank, straining to see into the distance. Again, he saw the flicker, like a tiny star in the middle of the hill, just beyond the edge of the town. Determined to find someone, anyone, who could tell him what the heck was going on, Evan jumped off the snowbank and began trotting down the empty street. His boots slapped the slushy sidewalk as he ran and his breath rang loud in his ears before it hung frozen in the still air.

He scanned the hillside for the flicker of light and continued to run toward it. Soon he arrived at the rocky base of a tall hill and began picking his way through a path among the rocks. As he looked up, trying to spot the light, he realized that there was a building on the top of the hill. Evan stared, his eyes wide. He could see towers rising on either side of an immense doorway. Tattered banners drooped from tall, narrow windows.

"It's a castle," he whispered.

He stopped climbing and turned around. Halfway up the

hill, he looked down at the empty town, darker still under the growing dusk. He shifted his gaze back to the once majestic castle, then to the oddly glassy sky. The scene seemed strangely familiar.

Then it hit him.

He frantically grabbed at his shoulders, feeling for the straps of his backpack. It wasn't there.

"I'm dreaming," he said out loud, pinching his arm as hard as he could. He squeezed his eyes shut, and then opened them.

He looked up—the castle still loomed above him. He looked down at the deserted village below. And he suddenly knew exactly where he was.

"I'm not dreaming," he exclaimed. "I'm inside the snow globe!"

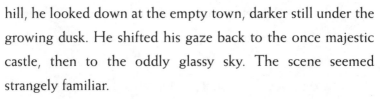

KNOWING WHERE he was didn't provide any comfort. Evan didn't even try to think how he could have ended up inside a Christmas decoration. Deep down, he knew that it was true. He also knew he needed to get out of the cold.

The dark and looming castle didn't look too inviting, so

Evan picked his way back down through the rocks, hoping to find someone, anyone, at home in the village.

Once down in the town, he wandered from door to door, knocking and calling out: "Anyone home? Hello?"

After about the tenth door, Evan was ready to give up hope.

"One more try," he muttered through chattering teeth, as he made his way up the sidewalk toward a small, neat, white cottage. Dark windows framed the doorway and Evan's breath frosted the panes as he leaned close to peer inside. There was no sign of life.

Without much hope, he lifted his fist and pounded it against the door, feeling pins and needles as his frozen hand knocked against the wood.

"Hello?" he called.

No answer.

"Is anybody home?"

The house remained silent.

In despair, weak from the cold, Evan leaned against the door. Slowly, silently, the door swung open. Evan staggered and caught his balance. Should he just go in? Was breaking and entering okay if you were freezing and lost?

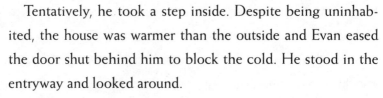

Tentatively, he took a step inside. Despite being uninhabited, the house was warmer than the outside and Evan eased the door shut behind him to block the cold. He stood in the entryway and looked around.

"Hello?" he said again, softly.

Evan slipped out of his boots, stamping his toes on the slate floor to warm his feet. Looking to his right, he saw a comfortable living room. An oversized sofa was pulled up in front of an empty fireplace. Overwhelmed with exhaustion, he made his way to the couch and lay down. A brightly colored plaid throw had been tossed over the arm of the couch, and he pulled it tightly around his shoulders.

Lying in the dark, he thought of his mom and dad and sisters. How long had he been gone? Did they even know he was missing yet? He closed his eyes tightly and pictured his own house. He saw the golden candlelight in the windows, the bright red ribbons on the wreaths. The house glowed with warmth and Christmas cheer. He could almost smell the gingerbread baking in the oven. Tears slid out from beneath his eyelids.

"I've got to get home," he said to the empty house. "I've got to get home for Christmas."

WITH A START, Evan bolted upright. For a minute he didn't know where he was. He realized he had fallen asleep. He had been dreaming of hiking through the woods to cut down the Christmas tree. As his father cut the trunk with his saw, the tree had teetered, then fallen to the snowy ground with a crash.

Evan shook his head. Trees landing in snow didn't crash. He crouched down on the couch, making himself as small as he could, and strained his ears in the silence.

Crash.

There it was again!

Thump. Creeeak. Thwap.

The sounds were coming from the kitchen.

Hoping that the family who lived here had returned, Evan got up from the couch and crept to the doorway.

Although it was noisy, there were no lights on in the kitchen. His heart pounding, Evan tiptoed down the hallway toward the noise. He peered around the kitchen doorway.

In the dim glow of the refrigerator light, Evan could see the silhouette of a short, thin figure. It looked like a kid, not much

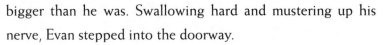
bigger than he was. Swallowing hard and mustering up his nerve, Evan stepped into the doorway.

"Excuse me," he said.

"Eeeyaaah!" screamed the figure, jumping back from the fridge and dropping an armload of cheese, bread, apples, and oranges. An orange rolled toward Evan and he leaned down to pick it up.

"Here," he said, holding it out. "Sorry, I didn't mean to startle you."

The figure inched closer and Evan could see that it was not a kid, but a very small man. His features were sharp, but kind. He was dressed in tattered clothing that looked like it had once been brightly colored, but was now faded and worn. He wore a long, tasseled stocking cap pulled down over his ears and odd boots with curling toes.

"Who are you?" the little man squeaked out.

"Evan Darling. I'm lost," Evan explained. "I'm sorry I just came into your house, but no one answered when I knocked."

"Well, of course no one answered," the little man said, beginning to pick the food up from the kitchen floor. "No one's home."

"You are," Evan pointed out.

"This isn't my home," he replied.

"Then what are you doing here?" Evan asked.

"What are *you* doing here?"

"I told you. I'm lost. I need help getting home."

"You're not from around here?" The little man stepped closer, studying Evan curiously.

"I live in Holidayle," Evan explained. "And by the way, where exactly is *here* anyway?"

"You don't know?"

Evan was getting a little tired of having his questions answered with questions. After all, he had a million questions himself. Like: What was up with the whole village in a snow globe thing? And where was everybody? And what was the story with the big castle on the hill?

"Look," he said, not caring if he sounded ridiculous. "I was running home in a snowstorm and the next thing I know I'm here, inside a snow globe. And I want to get home."

The little man grinned. His whole face lit up and Evan suddenly noticed he had sparkling blue eyes. "So you do know where you are."

The little man pulled out a kitchen chair and motioned for Evan to sit down.

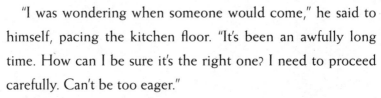

"I was wondering when someone would come," he said to himself, pacing the kitchen floor. "It's been an awfully long time. How can I be sure it's the right one? I need to proceed carefully. Can't be too eager."

"What do you mean, a long time? The right one?" Evan was growing more confused by the minute. "Look, Mr.—"

"Noel Christmastree, II," the little man said, grasping Evan's hand in his and shaking it vigorously.

"Well, Mr. Christmastree," Evan began.

"Please, most people call me Noel the Second."

"Why?"

"My dad was the First Noel." The little man waved his hand dismissively. "Aw, heck, just call me Noel."

"Can I ask you a question?" Evan said.

Noel nodded.

"What day is today?"

"December twenty-first," Noel answered.

Evan blinked in surprise. So he'd lost two days, somehow. Well, that was good, he told himself. He'd definitely be able to make it home in time for Christmas, now.

"And where is everyone?" Evan continued. "Shouldn't they all be here getting ready for Christmas?"

"Oh, they think they're getting ready for Christmas, all right." Then Noel muttered darkly, "Fools."

As Evan watched, the anger faded from the little man's face and his shoulders slumped. When he looked back up at Evan, his bright blue eyes looked dimmer somehow.

"They'll be home soon enough," he said glumly. "Right on December twenty-seventh. Like clockwork."

As soon as Noel said the word "home," Evan's curiosity about the strange town faded. Only one question mattered.

"How can I get home, Noel?" Evan asked.

"I don't have the answer to that, my young friend, but I know where you might inquire," Noel said mysteriously.

Evans hopes lifted. "Where?" he asked eagerly.

Noel walked toward the front door of the house, gesturing for Evan to follow. He went out on the porch and pointed to a rise on the other side of the town, opposite the castle.

Evan squinted into the darkness. Gradually he made out the outline of a low, square building squatting on a gentle hill just past all the houses. No warm, welcoming lights glowed from its windowless façade.

"Are you talking about that big ugly concrete building?" Evan asked. "What is it? The town police station or something?"

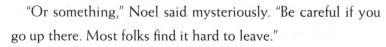
"Or something," Noel said mysteriously. "Be careful if you go up there. Most folks find it hard to leave."

Evan was so excited by the prospect of finding someone who could tell him how to get back home, that he barely said "Thank you" to Noel. He bounded off the porch.

"Hey, Evan," Noel called out. "Wait."

Evan turned as Noel came down the steps. Despite his funny shoes, he moved nimbly. He grasped Evan's wrist with one hand and gave him a folded piece of paper.

"Hang on to this. If you have any questions for me, just follow these directions. But don't let anyone see it." Noel's face and tone became serious. "And don't tell anyone you've met me."

Evan nodded. He didn't stop to wonder why Noel wanted to remain anonymous. He figured it had something to do with burgling the fridge in the house. Stuffing the piece of paper into his pocket, Evan began running down the dark and empty street toward the building that he hoped held the answers to his questions.

"Evan."

The third soldier brushed aside an unruly black beard and reached inside his blue tunic to pull out a huge clipboard. Evan peered at his nametag: *Sergeant Donner*. The man ran a finger down a list, flipping many pages as he did so. "Family name?" he asked gruffly.

"Darling," Evan said.

"What'd he call you?" Dasher elbowed Donner in the ribs. "Sounds like you two know each other already."

Dasher and Blitzen snorted with laughter as Donner flushed so red, his cheek spots disappeared.

"Don't be smart with me," Donner sputtered at Evan, his beard moving furiously as he spoke. "Give me your family name, or it's off to the Sheriff with you."

"Who are you guys?" Evan asked. "And what's with the costumes and the reindeer names? Is this some kind of a Christmas pageant? Am I backstage or something?"

"Oh, a real wise man, eh?" Donner sneered.

The three officers stared at Evan. Finally the one in green spoke. "He could be a spy."

The others nodded their agreement. "I think we should take him straight to the Sheriff," the one in red said firmly.

Four

HIS BOOTS slapping loudly on the pavement, Evan kept up a brisk trot past all the empty houses. He followed the curving path of the roadway, which seemed to have been recently plowed. Before long, Noel and the small, silent village were behind him.

He slowed to a walk as he approached the building. He was

just taking it easy while he caught his breath, he told himself. But the building seemed foreboding, and Evan wondered fleetingly if this was really where he would find help in getting home.

He walked slowly around the outside of the building. He had been right; there were no windows. The cinder-block walls were unpainted and the snow had piled high against their bare sides.

"Doesn't seem like there's anyone up here, either," he muttered as he trudged along the perimeter, looking for a way in.

Suddenly, he heard a noise. It was muffled and faint, and Evan strained his ears to be sure. As he crept around the corner, he heard it more clearly. The strains of "Jingle Bells" were seeping out of the cement walls.

Evan's heart jumped. It was nearly Christmas here, too. He was sure to find someone who could help him return to his family.

Moving toward the source of the music, he saw the faint outline of a door etched into the wall in front of him. He marched up to the shadowy entry and raised his hand to knock.

But as he moved his hand forward, the rows of cinder block suddenly slid apart, leaving a doorway framed by their ragged edges. Before Evan could step in, a hand shot out and gripped his arm in an iron grasp, and yanked him into the building.

"Well, well, well. What have we got here?"

Evan was speechless. The man before him was d soldier from *The Nutcracker*. Every Christmas, another part in the performance and every Christ could remember, Evan's mother had dragged h ballet. This year Elyse had been in it, too.

The man held Evan at arm's length and studi Evan stared back. The man wore white pants black boots, which were topped with a re nearly to his knees. His green tunic was hi broad epaulets and elaborate gold embroider his hips with a wide piece of leather. The thick, red beard and bright red spots pain On his head rested a tall green hat trim adorned with white plumes above the shir

Officer Dasher, read the nametag over hi

"Looks like we've got a latecomer," (over his shoulder, as two more men in th running up.

"What's your name, boy?" asked one with a bushy white beard and a brigh read *Officer Blitzen*.

"Hey, who are you guys?" Evan asked again as he found himself lifted off the ground, an officer gripping under his arm on each side. "I just want to know how to go home."

The men exchanged grim glances, but didn't speak.

Evan glanced back at the opening in the wall. "Maybe I should just go ask directions somewhere else."

"Don't pretend you don't know the rules," Dasher snarled, gripping his right arm.

"Yeah," Blitzen said, grabbing tightly to his left arm. "No one leaves the Christmas Complex until the Twelve Days of Christmas are over."

Donner unclipped a small device that looked very much like an automatic garage door opener from his belt. Pointing it at the wall, he pressed a big red button. As Evan stared in amazement and dismay, the walls slid shut, the cinder blocks interlocking smoothly. From the inside, there was no sign of a door.

The officers moved briskly through what seemed to be a short tunnel, talking as if Evan wasn't even there.

"First humbug we've caught all year," Dasher said.

"Thought we'd gotten rid of all of them," Blitzen agreed. "I've never seen such a young one, though."

"It's already the seventh day. How do you suppose he stayed

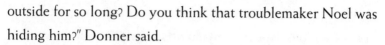

outside for so long? Do you think that troublemaker Noel was hiding him?" Donner said.

"The Sheriff will get the answers out of him," Blitzen said confidently. He gave an impatient tug on Evan's arm. "Let's just get him to the office as quietly as possible."

Donner pushed a green button on the wall at the end of the tunnel and two huge metal doors swung slowly inward. The foursome stepped out of the tunnel and Evan's mouth dropped in shock.

It was as if they had stepped into the middle of the most crowded shopping mall in the world. But this was no ordinary mall, Evan realized. From the paper snowflakes dangling from a network of pipes crossing the ceiling high above, to the design of bows and ivy on the carpet under his feet, the entire building was decked out for Christmas. Loudspeakers hung from the walls, piping the sweet melodies of Christmas carols over the bustling crowd.

People carrying armloads of packages rushed back and forth, sometimes bumping into each other in their haste. Parents rushed from store to store, clutching red-faced children by the wrist. Cries of "Happy Holidays" and "Merry Christmas" filled the air.

Evan's gaze drifted along a row of shops. Outside of one, a man dressed as a snowman stood on a box shouting through a megaphone, "Step right up, step right up. Don't be the only ones on the block without your own snow-making machine. That's right. You can enjoy the pleasures of winter sports twelve months a year with this handy high-tech H_2O crystallizer. Only a limited number will be sold this year, so get yours now!"

People who had crowded around the snowman began shoving their way into the store, waving their credit cards above their heads.

"Gotta get me one of those," Blitzen muttered, following Evan's gaze. "I hate the heat."

Just then the sound of sleigh bells filled the air.

"Say, I think it looks like snow!" the loudspeakers blared heartily. White flakes began to fall from the pipes on the ceiling, landing gently on Evan's forehead. They were cold and white. They felt just like real snow.

"Better get in out of the weather," the loudspeakers advised jovially. "The Christmas Sock Shop has a two-for-one special that you won't want to miss."

"Let's get moving," Donner said, giving Evan a little shove.

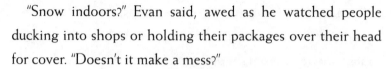

"Snow indoors?" Evan said, awed as he watched people ducking into shops or holding their packages over their head for cover. "Doesn't it make a mess?"

"Don't act like you've never seen it before. We added this seasonal feature two years ago," Donner said. "Besides, the Complex temperature is kept at a comfortable sixty-eight degrees for maximum shopping pleasure. The snow melts before it hits the ground."

Evan caught the eye of a kindly looking woman who was resting on a bench, an umbrella held up against the flakes, a huge pile of shopping bags at her feet.

"Help, please, could you help me?" He struggled to break free of the soldiers on either side of him.

The woman looked at the group quizzically.

"Pay no attention to him, ma'am," Donner said. "Potential humbug. We're just taking him in for some questioning."

"I'm just trying to get home," Evan said, desperately.

"See what we mean?" Blitzen said, saluting smartly with his free hand. "Happy Holidays, ma'am."

The woman stood up and nodded. Without a word to Evan, she closed her umbrella and picked up her bags. No one else stopped to look at them as Evan and his escorts moved steadily through the complex.

After walking past stores, restaurants, and video arcades, all featuring Christmas-themed wares and activities, the officers stopped in front of a huge door painted candy cane red-and-white. The doorway was festooned with silver tinsel and flanked by a pair of huge reindeer lawn ornaments—the kind covered in white lights. In the middle of the door was a golden plaque, polished to a high shine. OFFICE, PRIVATE, DO NOT ENTER, THAT MEANS YOU! read the sign.

"Time to talk to the Boss," Officer Donner said to Evan. He reached his hand toward the doorknob.

"Oh, *there* you are," a voice behind them said loudly. Evan and the officers all jumped and whirled around.

A girl was standing in front of them, smiling broadly, her hands stuck casually in her pants pockets. She looked like she was about Evan's age. Taking one hand out of her pocket, she pushed a mop of unruly brown curls out of her face, then reached out toward Evan. "I thought you'd never get here."

"Do I . . ." Evan began.

She raised one eyebrow at him. *Play along with me,* her eyes seemed to say.

"I guess I'm . . . er, a little late, huh?" Evan said.

"You know this boy?" Officer Donner frowned at the girl.

" 'Course I do, Officer Donner," she said brightly. "It's—"

"Ev-an," Evan mouthed silently.

"—my cousin Evan," she finished smoothly. "He was travel-ing up from Grandma's to get here for the Twelve Days. Was there a storm or something, Evan?"

"Yes, yes," Evan said gratefully. "A tremendous storm. Very hard to travel. I really don't know how I got here at all."

Officer Blitzen frowned. "He was giving us a load of Hum-bug when we first found him."

"Oh, I'm sure he was just joking. Weren't you, Evan?" The girl had moved closer and taken Evan's hand. Now she stepped slowly back, leading Evan away from the officers and the doorway. "Dad is always on him about that. Isn't he, Evan?"

Evan just nodded his head yes. He wasn't sure what was going on, but if he was getting out of meeting the Sheriff, he was all for it.

"All right, then, Merry." Officer Donner nodded his head slowly. "We'll let him go with you." He glared at Evan. "But you better watch out. If we hear of one more incident . . ." His voice trailed off in a threatening way.

"I'll be sure to tell Dad how helpful you were, making sure

he got in safely and all," the girl said smiling sweetly. "C'mon, Evan"—tugging at his arm, urgently now. "Mom's waiting." She led him quickly away from the three men, leaving them standing at the office door.

The girl moved ahead of him. She kept glancing back over her shoulder and changed direction several times. Every time Evan started to ask her a question, she held her finger to her lips as if to tell him to be quiet. Finally they turned away from the shopping throngs and made their way down a long corridor, lit by fluorescent red-and-green lights.

The corridor ended in an open atrium with a huge, decorated Christmas tree in the center. Evan gave a low whistle. The tree was thirty feet tall, at least. He wondered how they managed to cut it down and drag it in, but then realized that the tree was artificial. He moved closer, sniffing. There was no scent of fresh pine, and up close he could see that the decorations consisted of glass balls bearing the names of the stores in the Complex. The shimmering silver decorations that dangled from nearly every branch were thousands of tiny dollar signs.

Evan looked away from the tree. There were no shops in this part of the Complex, which rose up three stories. On each

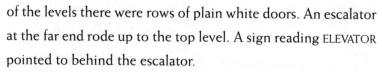

of the levels there were rows of plain white doors. An escalator at the far end rode up to the top level. A sign reading ELEVATOR pointed to behind the escalator.

"Where are we?" he blurted out.

"Home," Merry said simply. "Everyone stays in the Christmas Condos during the Twelve Days."

She jumped on the escalator, taking the moving stairs two at a time. Evan followed her. On the third floor, she hopped off and made her way down to the last door. The long corridors were silent and empty.

"Where is everyone?" Evan asked, feeling a horrible sense of déjà vu.

"Shopping, of course." Merry reached into her pocket and pulled out what looked like a credit card and slid it into a slot next to the door. The door opened with a *whoosh* and she stepped inside. When Evan hesitated, she reached her hand out and pulled him through the doorway.

Evan was surprised to find himself in a very comfortable living room.

Merry sat down on a big red-and-green plaid sofa.

"I've got a million questions," they said at the same time.

"You go first," they said in stereo.

"Company first," Merry said, kicking her sneakers off and pulling her legs up underneath her. "You ask three questions, then I'll ask three." She impatiently brushed a dark curl out of her eyes and leaned forward, elbows on her knees, looking at Evan expectantly.

Evan couldn't sit down. Here, in the quiet of a perfectly normal-looking living room, the strangeness of his situation hit him full force.

He shrugged out of his coat and kicked off his boots and began to pace.

"Okay, well, first of all, who *were* those guys and why did you save me?"

"They're called the Police Navidad—the security guards here at the Complex. They're jerks, real big bullies with nothing to do," she said. "And I saved you from them 'cuz I could. Believe me, you do not want to meet the Sheriff!"

"How come they listened to you?"

Merry blushed. "My dad's their boss," she said. "Captain Kringle."

"So he's like the Captain of the Police Force?" Evan felt a flare of optimism. Maybe he had found someone who could help him get home after all. "Is he a jerk like those other guys?"

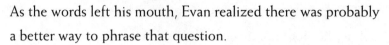

As the words left his mouth, Evan realized there was probably a better way to phrase that question.

But to his great surprise, Merry didn't get angry. A sad expression flitted across her face. "He's a jerk for taking the job," she said. "But he's not like the others. At least, he didn't used to be. And that's four questions. So now it's my turn."

Evan flopped down in a green leather recliner across from her and nodded his assent.

"How come you were late getting to the Complex?" she asked.

"Well, I sort of just got into town . . ." Evan said. Now it was his turn to blush. If he told this girl the truth, she was going to think he was a big fat liar.

"You don't live in the village. And that's a statement, not one of my questions," she pointed out quickly.

"No, I don't live in the village," Evan said. "In fact, I'm trying to get home."

"No wonder you didn't know about the Complex," she said thoughtfully. "Don't you have one where you're from? How the heck do you celebrate Christmas without a Complex?"

"We don't have one, and we have all kinds of traditions," Evan said. He yawned widely, suddenly overcome with exhaustion. It had been a long, strange night. His eyes were growing heavy and he blinked hard, trying to keep them open.

"You can stay here if you want," Merry said. "I've got bunk beds. You can have the top." She led Evan down a short hallway and into a small, cluttered room. Rows of shopping bags lined one wall and wrapped boxes were lying in a festive heap on the top bunk. "We can talk more in the morning, after the others have gone out."

"The others?" Evan asked.

"My mom, my dad, and my twin sisters, Holly and Ivy," Merry explained. "They'll all be home soon." Her expression was thoughtful. "Maybe it's better if they don't know you're here—'specially my dad."

She clambered up the ladder and shifted the boxes on the top bed around so that there was a little nest in the center. Moving to the side of the ladder, she motioned for Evan to climb up. He crawled into the space between the boxes and gratefully lay down. As he pulled a blanket up around his shoulders, he was barely aware of the light layer of cardboard boxes and gift wrap that Merry piled on top of him.

Five

"WAKE UP SHOPPERS—ONLY TWO MORE SHOPPING
DAYS 'TIL CHRISTMAS!"

Somewhere above Evan's head, a loudspeaker blared. He
mumbled and pulled his blanket up over his ears. He'd been
having the strangest dream. . . .

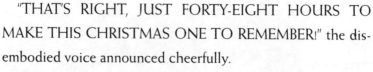

"THAT'S RIGHT, JUST FORTY-EIGHT HOURS TO MAKE THIS CHRISTMAS ONE TO REMEMBER!" the disembodied voice announced cheerfully.

Evan snapped awake, sitting up so suddenly that he bumped his head on the low ceiling above the bunk. A cascade of gift boxes tumbled over the side, thumping to the floor. As he was trying to figure out where he was, Merry's face appeared at the edge of the bed. Evan's heart sank as he realized it was no dream.

"Quiet, everyone's still home," she hissed.

She whirled around at the sound of footsteps outside her room.

"Merry?" a woman's voice called out from the other side of the door.

Evan ducked back under the covers, trying not to make any noise as Merry began heaving the boxes back on top of him.

"Sorry, Mom," Merry said. "I was trying to find something and knocked over my gift stack."

The door to the room opened a crack.

"No, Mom! Don't! Don't come in! I don't want to ruin your Christmas surprise."

Evan held his breath.

"Oh, how sweet. All right, dear. Just make sure you meet us at one o'clock at the Family Portrait Studio. We've got our appointment for our annual Christmas photo. Don't forget: Wear the Christmas tree sweater. Your father wants to commemorate the most profitable sales season ever."

"Okay, Mom. See you at one." Merry eased the door shut with a sigh of relief.

"You can come out now," she whispered.

"We all had to wear the same sweaters for our family photo, too," Evan said sympathetically as he climbed down from the bunk. "But what did your mom mean when she said it would remind your dad of a profitable sales season?"

"You really don't know anything about Christmas, do you?" Merry said wonderingly. "Christmas trees were invented from the shape of a fourth quarter sales graph."

She grabbed a piece of paper and a green crayon. Starting in the left-hand corner, she began to draw. "The Twelve Days start, and sales go up, and up, and up." She zigged and zagged a green line to the top of the page. "Until Christmas Day." She grabbed a yellow crayon and drew a big star on the top, then held the paper up for Evan to see. He had to admit, it did look like a Christmas tree.

"Uh, I'm not sure that's really how Christmas trees were invented," Evan said.

"How, then?" Merry looked at him defiantly.

"They were . . . that is, you cut them down, because, er . . . Y'know, I'm really hungry." Evan didn't want to admit he had no idea why.

"We can go get something to eat in the Complex," Merry said. "And I'll tell you more about the Christmas traditions. We've got lots."

She smiled. "It's kind of fun having someone new to share them with. It can be kind of boring when your family makes you do the same thing over and over every year, you know?"

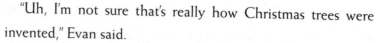

EVAN WAS SITTING at a table in the Christmas Feast restaurant with Merry, shoveling in food as fast as he could. He'd ordered a Three French Henwich, Golden Onion Rings, and a Chocolate Maids a'Milking Shake. It was the best breakfast he'd ever had. He took one last slurp of his drink and leaned back in his chair.

"So what's with everything being named after Christmas around here, anyway?" he asked Merry.

Merry smiled indulgently. "I can see that I have to start at the beginning," she said. "I can't believe you don't celebrate Christmas."

"But I do," Evan protested.

"Well, maybe so," Merry allowed. "But it's not very traditional. There are Twelve Days of Christmas, starting on December fifteenth—that's the first day of The Big Sellout. We all close up our houses in the village and come up here to the Christmas Complex, where we do all our shopping and see Christmas shows and have Christmas contests, like a beauty pageant to pick Miss Yuletide Carol. My sisters won last year. It was the first time there was ever a tie. The Sellout Celebration goes all the way until late at night on December twenty-fourth. Then, on the twenty-fifth we wake up early and all the families gather together and go through all the stuff they've bought. We sort it out into things we want to keep and things we need to exchange. Then, the twelfth day of Christmas is the twenty-sixth. That's when everything really goes on sale. It's the craziest day of the year. And after that, the Police Navidad open the doors to the

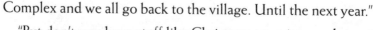

Complex and we all go back to the village. Until the next year."

"But don't you have stuff like Christmas trees in your house? Or stockings hung by the fire? Or Christmas carolers who go out at night and sing in front of your house?" Evan desperately tried to find some common tradition he and Merry shared.

Merry looked at him strangely. "Why would anyone bring a tree into the house?" she asked. Then her face brightened. "But we do hang stockings by the fire. Everyone knows that warm stockings are the best cure for mistletoe."

At the word "mistletoe," Evan made a face. Of all the common traditions . . .

Merry looked sympathetic. "I know, my dad always gets the worst case every year. It's from having to patrol the Complex all day. But we just keep a pair of wool stockings hanging by the fire, and every night he comes home and slips his aching feet into the toasty socks. The next morning, his mistletoe is much better."

Evan burst out laughing. "Mistletoe's not some kind of foot fungus," he snorted. "It's a plant and you bring it inside and then people kiss under it."

"Why would you do that?" It was Merry's turn to laugh. "Why would anyone have such a ridiculous custom?"

Evan scratched his head. Why indeed?

When he didn't answer, Merry stood up. "You've got some weird ideas about Christmas," she said, fighting back giggles. "We'd better get going. I've got to do some shopping before I meet my family. They'll be suspicious if I don't have any packages."

Evan followed her back into the neon glare of the Complex. Red and green klieg lights spun their beams crazily off the ceiling. Outside of the stores, men dressed like carnival barkers stood above the crowd, trying to lure them into the shops.

"Step right up, step right up. Get your gold-plated toenail clippers right here. Last chance to purchase the ultimate luxury item. Only 150 in stock. Don't be left out."

Evan whipped his head from side to side, taking it all in. He noticed several of the Police Navidad strolling through the mall, nodding approval at the shoppers laden with packages.

A banner in a store selling beds announced: GOOD REST YE MERRY GENTLEMEN.

A small boy walking past tugged his mother's arm, pulling her toward a pet shop where fat red puppies frolicked in the window. "Look Mama, Pointsetter puppies! Please, can I get one, Mama? Please?"

Evan studied the faces of the crowd rushing past him. No one looked happy. They all looked pretty frazzled, in fact. He imagined twelve days worth of Christmas preparation and shuddered. He thought about how his family rushed around like crazy right up until Christmas Eve, but then, how still and magical the house became as everyone awaited the wonder of Christmas Day.

"Merry, do you really like Christmas?" Evan asked abruptly, feeling suddenly sorry for her.

"What kind of a weird question is that?" Merry stopped walking and stared at him.

"Do you like it?" he pressed.

"'Course I like it," she said. Then looking away, a wistful expression on her face, she dropped her voice to a whisper. "Only sometimes I wish . . ."

Evan leaned in closer to hear her.

"What, what do you wish?" His face was so close to hers, he could see that her green eyes were flecked with gold.

"Hey Merry, who's your boyfriend?" Two teenage girls with long blond hair appeared out of the crowd.

Merry jumped back from Evan, blushing furiously. "This is my *friend*, Evan," she said pointedly. "Evan, these are my sisters, Holly and Ivy."

The two teenagers smiled at him, revealing perfect white

teeth. They tossed their hair back over their shoulders at the same time, then carefully smoothed it down. They reminded Evan of his sister Kelly.

"I don't think I've seen you hanging around before," one of the twins said.

Evan studied them closely. He really couldn't tell them apart at all.

"He's kind of new to the Complex," Merry said evasively.

"Actually I'm trying to get home in time for Christmas," Evan explained.

Merry shot him a dirty look.

"Dude, you're right in the middle of Christmas," said Holly—or was it Ivy?

"Where I'm from, Christmas is only on December twenty-fifth," Evan said. "We don't really do this whole pre-Christmas extravaganza. Well, we sort of do, but it's not really, truly Christmas. It's just—sort of—you know, preparation."

"You're talking like a Humbug," one of the twins said.

"He's not a Humbug, Ivy," Merry said hotly, glancing around as if someone might hear.

"Takes one to know one," Holly taunted. "Maybe that's why you like hanging around with him."

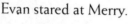

Evan stared at Merry.

"Well, maybe I've heard about something like what you are talking about," she said defensively. "And I do think it sounds kind of nice . . ."

"Better not let Dad hear you say that," Holly said.

"Yeah," Ivy continued. "You know how he is about tradition. And speaking of traditions, are you going to come and watch the pageant?"

"We're a cinch to win the Miss Yuletide Carol," Holly said. "Wait 'til you see what we're doing for the talent portion!"

The twins exchanged a glance and broke into giggles, tossing their hair again and preening. They had clearly lost interest in Merry, Evan, or further discussions about Christmas.

"Wanna watch?" Merry looked at Evan.

"Sure," he said shrugging.

E V A N A N D M E R R Y lagged behind the twins as they made their way through the Complex. Evan wanted to ask Merry more about how she really felt about Christmas, but she kept chattering about the traditions in the Complex. She pointed out the tiny boxing ring where a family, dressed in boxing trunks and protective gear, sat under a gaudy banner proclaiming: "Deck the Halls—$5.00 per Round." She dragged Evan into a perfume store so she could buy some Joy Eau de Noel for her mom, and into a florist shop where she asked the florist for a Wreath of Franklins. Evan watched the woman quickly fashion a wreath out of folded five-dollar bills. She tied it with a huge red bow and held it up for Merry's inspection.

"It's great. Dad will love it," she said, asking the woman to charge it to Captain Kringle's account.

"So, Merry—" Evan began as they walked out of the shop.

"Oh my gosh! We're going to be late for the pageant," Merry exclaimed. She started jogging down the Complex.

"Okay, I can take a hint," Evan puffed, trying to keep up with her. "You don't want to talk about it."

Merry skidded to a stop so quickly that Evan nearly tripped over her. They had arrived at a huge stage, decorated in bright lights and tinsel, which dominated one end of the Complex. Spotlights were set to shine in front of the heavy red velvet curtain that was drawn across the front.

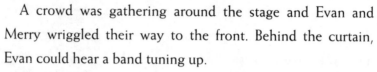

A crowd was gathering around the stage and Evan and Merry wriggled their way to the front. Behind the curtain, Evan could hear a band tuning up.

Merry had stopped her running commentary for the moment and Evan seized his chance. "Did you mean what you said, back there?" he whispered. "About Christmas?"

She nodded, looking around nervously. "We can't talk about it here. But after this, I have something I want to show you."

An announcer, with slicked-back black hair and dressed in a red velvet tuxedo, stepped out from behind the curtain. The crowd applauded.

"Welcome to our annual extravaganza of song, dance, and beauty," he began. "Our contestants are the most beautiful young ladies here at the Christmas Complex. But only the most talented, the most poised, the most full of Christmas cheer, will be named Miss Yuletide Carol!"

The crowd roared its approval. Merry rolled her eyes. "I would *never*," she whispered to Evan.

"And so now, without further ado, I present our first con- testants." The announcer gestured dramatically toward the curtain. "Holly and Ivy!"

The curtains swept back slowly to reveal a full orchestra set up on risers. The musicians were dressed in red-and-white striped blazers and green trousers. They reminded Evan of a TV special from Las Vegas that he had to watch with his grandmother last time she visited.

The band struck up a tune, which Evan immediately recognized as "Here We Come a'Wassailing." The familiar melody reassured him. Maybe here, at last, was the kind of Christmas tradition he could identify with.

From the wings there was a sudden load roar, and to Evan's astonishment, a band of leather-clad motorcyclists zoomed out onto the stage.

"What's up with the bikers?" Evan said. "Where are your sisters?"

"I'm afraid that the bikers are their backup singers," Merry said. "They're the Harold's Angels. They sing every year at Christmas."

As Evan watched, Holly and Ivy jumped off the backs of two motorcycles and pranced to center stage. They were wearing headset microphones and outfits that looked like they had raided Britney Spears's Christmas closet.

"Oooh, Dad's gonna kill them," Merry muttered; then she grinned. "This is gonna be great."

Striking mirror poses, Holly and Ivy launched into an upbeat number.

> *Here we come a'cycling among the red and green*
> *Here we come a'cycling the coolest to be seen.*

The bikers all joined in on the refrain:

> *Babes and brew come to you, and a wicked tattoo too*
> *And we wish you will spend to increase the profit here.*
> *And spend to increase the profit here. . . .*

The song ended and Holly and Ivy hopped on the back of the two biggest choppers and waved gaily as they roared off the stage. The crowd went wild, stamping their feet and hooting.

Evan and Merry slipped toward the back, sneaking past a tall man in an impressive gold uniform who was staring at the stage with a stony look on his face.

Evan felt Merry's elbow in his ribs. "That's Dad," she said under her breath. "Probably not a good time for you to meet him, though."

They scrunched down even lower and wormed their way out of the crowd.

"What did you want to show me?" Evan asked when they had reached a relatively quiet area.

"Promise you won't tell?" Merry asked.

"I promise."

Merry moved down another corridor, trotting briskly. They passed rows and rows of shops until they arrived at a rather plain storefront. Once inside, Evan realized that it was a post office. Harried workers rushed past them with overstuffed letter bags. Mail carriers ran in and out, stuffing handfuls of mail into their pouches before dashing off.

They moved past huge bins marked "Level One, Level Two, Level Three, and Confiscated."

"What's 'confiscated' mail?" Evan asked.

"Mail that's addressed to people outside of the Complex," Merry replied. "We're only supposed to send Christmas cards to the families that live here."

"Don't you have any family that lives outside of here—even during Christmastime?" Evan wondered.

"That's what I want to show you." Merry stopped in front of a bulletin board in the back of the post office. "Look."

Evan's gaze followed her pointing finger. He was looking at an enormous WANTED poster in full color.

"WANTED for Violation of the Christmas Spirit," he read. "REWARD for capture, Dead or Alive."

"I don't get it," he said.

The man in the picture certainly didn't look like any kind of a criminal. He was older, with wrinkles creasing his kindly face. He had a thick white beard and was wearing an old-fashioned cloak trimmed with thick, white fur.

"Read the name," Merry told him.

"Kris Kringle," Evan said. "No way! You want to arrest Santa Claus?"

"There's no such thing as Santa Claus," Merry said sadly. "No one just gives presents away. You've got to buy them. You're looking at my great-great grandfather."

"If your great-great grandfather is Santa Claus," Evan said, stubbornly emphasizing "Santa Claus," "how come your dad's part of the Police Navidad? Shouldn't the Christmas Spirit be in your family?"

"You're going to get us in trouble," Merry said, shushing him. "If the Sheriff hears you and decides we're Humbugs, he'll throw us out of the Complex or something. Anyway, my dad is

Captain because his dad was. I guess my grandpa's greatest wish was that his son would carry on the family tradition. Besides, my dad loves his job. The other night, I heard him talking to my mom. He was saying that he felt like *he* was The Big Sellout. So, it must mean a lot to him, right?"

"Where's your great-great grandfather now?" Evan asked.

"No one knows," Merry said. "He'd be very old. Or maybe he's dead. No one's ever survived a Christmas outside of the Complex."

She was white and shaking with fear, and Evan realized what it had cost her to share her secret with him. He also realized that he did, in fact, know someone who was surviving a Christmas outside of the Complex.

"Okay, I'll keep quiet about it," Evan told her, relieved to see some color coming back into her face as they left. He hoped she was feeling better, because there was something he had to do. And do alone. "Hey, don't you have to go meet your parents for photos?"

"Oh my gosh!" Merry began raking her fingers through her unruly curls. "I totally forgot. Listen, Evan, I can hide you again if you want. Or if my dad's recovered from my sisters' performance, maybe I can introduce you to him. He's not a bad guy, really. Maybe he'll help you get home after we leave the Complex."

"Maybe," Evan said noncommittally, his fingers already wrapped around the scrap of paper in his pocket. "I'll just look around a bit. Is there somewhere I can meet you later?"

"We can meet under the Christmas tree in the atrium," she said. "If you go right underneath it, kind of in the branches, you can look up at all the lights." Her voice turned dreamy. "They twinkle like stars, you know."

"I do know," Evan said softly.

Waving good-bye to his new friend, he strolled down another garish corridor as casually as he could. Ducking behind a huge plastic candy cane archway, he pulled the crumpled piece of paper out of his pocket and, smoothing it down, began to study it.

Six

THE PAPER SHOWED a crude diagram of the Complex. Evan turned it this way and that, trying to get his bearings. There were arrows pointing at various spots along the outside walls. Next to each arrow were the tiny words, Aire Vent. He studied the map again. How was he supposed to know how to get to these aire vents? As he squinted, more words came into focus. "You are here," it said next to a tiny dot. As the layout of the Complex became clear to him, Evan realized that one of the arrows was right over the area marked "stage."

He retraced his steps to where he and Merry had watched her sisters just a few hours before. The stage was empty and dark and the crowd had dispersed long ago. Moving quickly, Evan boosted himself onto the stage and went behind one of the enormous curtains. Just as he was about to dash across the stage to the scaffolding behind the band riser, he heard voices.

He ducked back into the voluminous folds of the stage curtains.

Several of the band members ambled onto the stage.

"I can't believe we have to rehearse again today," one muttered, seating himself at a massive keyboard. "We were great at the pageant."

"It wasn't my idea," a guitar player said, sitting down in one of the folding chairs to tune his instrument.

"Whose idea was it?" The bass player plugged into his amp and began warming up.

"Who do you think?" The guitar player shrugged. "The only guy who's late."

"There's nothing worse than a drummer who can't keep track of the time," the bass player grumbled.

"What? Are we still waiting for the little drummer boy to show up?" A few more guys wandered onstage and took their places behind sheet music.

The horn section, Evan realized. He was beginning to sweat. How was he going to get off the stage, never mind up to the vents, with all those guys here? He peered out from the curtain, scanning for anything he might be able to climb.

"Let's get the show on the road!"

Evan sank back into the folds of the curtain as a red-haired figure jogged across the stage and hopped behind the drum kit.

The band kicked into an easy version of "White Christmas" and for a moment, Evan just enjoyed the music. Without any of the crazy mixed-up lyrics of the other Christmas songs he'd heard all day, the crooning melody was familiar and comforting. His whole body relaxed as he listened, and with the relaxation came a sudden inspiration: He knew how he could get to the top of the stage.

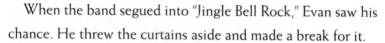

When the band segued into "Jingle Bell Rock," Evan saw his chance. He threw the curtains aside and made a break for it.

"Drum solo!" he yelled as he dashed across the stage, past the musicians and out of sight into the wings.

"Woohoo!" the drummer yelled back, his hair and sticks flailing.

Evan shimmied up the lighting scaffolding, the crashing cymbals masking the noise of his climb.

From the top of the scaffold, Evan could see an aire vent in the wall a few feet below the ceiling. Spotting a coiled rope attached to a sandbag, Evan picked it up, twirled it above his head like a lariat, and sent it flying toward a thick pipe running along the ceiling. He gave the rope a tug. Satisfied it was secure, he tied one end around his waist and prepared to swing across the narrow chasm between the scaffold and the grate in the wall.

"One. Two." He took a deep breath and closed his eyes.

"Three," said a voice below him as Evan felt fingers wrap around his ankle.

DONNER AND BLITZEN stood on either side of Evan, holding tight to his arms as they dragged him through the doorway of the Sheriff's office.

Once inside, Evan gazed around the room in amazement. Two of the four walls were covered with large color TV screens, each tuned to a different image. A third wall had a giant ticker tape that was constantly scrolling huge neon green letters: earrings 59.95 . . . silk scarf 68.00 . . . mountain bike 250.00 . . . toaster oven 35.98 . . . Let's Shop Barbie 14.95. . . . Evan realized it was a list of each purchase being made in the Complex. As he watched, the screen blinked and in bright red flashed: Total Sales $915,678.

A huge leather sofa stretched across the fourth wall. As his eyes adjusted to the dark of the room and the glare of the screens, Evan could barely make out the Sheriff's wiry frame nearly hidden among the pillows. Bowls of popcorn, half-eaten candy canes, a tin of sugarplums, and a plate of ginger-bread men lay on the coffee table in front of him.

The Sheriff had his eyes glued to the TV screens, and was using a giant remote control to zoom in on particular images. Scowling at the wall of monitors, he reached for a walkie-talkie lying next to him on the couch.

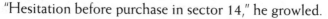
"Hesitation before purchase in sector 14," he growled.

Evan followed his gaze to the wall and saw a woman holding up an elaborate china figurine. He couldn't tell, but it looked like a unicorn. She turned it over in her hand, scrutinizing the price, and then, with a frown, replaced it on the shelf. Evan watched as her hand hovered in the air as if to pick it up again. A smiling salesclerk approached and after an animated conversation, the woman nodded, picked up the statue and trotted off toward the checkout counter. He could see the smug smile on the face of the salesperson as she turned away from the camera's view.

"Why some people have to be coaxed into the Christmas Spirit, I'll never know," the Sheriff muttered to himself. He finally turned his attention to the trio who had been standing in front of him.

"Hey boss, look who we found poking around backstage at the band rehearsal," Blitzen announced.

Evan kept his gaze steady as the Sheriff fixed him with a black, beady-eyed stare.

"Looking for something special?" the Sheriff asked innocently as he got to his feet.

"Uh, I thought I'd get my mom a present. Umm, yeah, a guitar—er, well, that is, I thought I'd ask the guys in the band where to *buy* one, because I don't remember seeing a music store. . . ." Evan shrugged free of Donner and Blitzen's grip. "Then these two dragged me in here."

"Shopping for your mom, were you?" the Sheriff said, his voice sweet. "Now that's a good boy. You're sure you're telling the truth? Because," he gestured to the wall of monitors, "I'd know if you were lying."

Behind Evan, Donner and Blitzen broke into song:

> *You better watch out, you better just buy*
> *You better just shop, we're telling you why*
> *Sheriff Klaws is watching you now. . . .*
> *He sees you when you're sleeping*
> *He knows when you're awake*
> *He knows if you've . . .*

"All right, all right," the Sheriff made a slashing motion. "Thank you, Backstreet Boys."

He turned to Evan with a smug look on his face. "But they're right, you know. I've been keeping an eye on you since you turned up here, and I've been meaning to have a little talk with

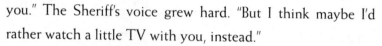

you." The Sheriff's voice grew hard. "But I think maybe I'd rather watch a little TV with you, instead."

Raising his remote, he pointed it at one of the screens: The scene shifted to the desolate snowy landscape outside of the Complex. He pushed another button and a small figure trudging up the hill toward the castle came into view.

Noel! Evan realized.

"Anyone you know?" The Sheriff leaned in menacingly and Evan could smell the candy cane on his breath.

"What? Out there?" Evan said innocently. "How could I know anyone out there?"

"Oh, you'd be surprised how many people you know show up on these screens," the Sheriff said. "Take a look."

The Sheriff pointed the remote at the wall of screens again and clicked. Suddenly every screen on the wall went black. The Sheriff clicked the remote again and images of Evan's family flooded the room.

"Mom, Dad!" Evan blurted out before he could help himself.

His mother and father were struggling through fiercely blowing snow. His mom clutched the collar of her coat tightly at her neck. "Evan," she called, her voice choked with fear. "Evan, where are you, honey?"

His dad held on to his mom's elbow, snow dusting his hair. "Let's go ask at the shops downtown again," he said. "I'm sure someone's seen him."

"I'm right here, Mom," Evan called, oblivious to Donner and Blitzen's snickers behind him.

The Sheriff clicked again and Evan's sisters appeared.

Kelly and Elyse were sitting on the edge of the bed in his room. He could see Elyse had been crying.

"Is Evan going to be home for Christmas?" she asked, looking up at Kelly.

"Sure he is," Kelly said.

" 'Cuz I don't want to have Christmas if he's not here," Elyse said, starting to sniffle. "If Santa would bring Evan home for Christmas, he wouldn't even have to bring me any toys. It just won't be Christmas without all of us together." She burst into tears.

"Mom and Dad will find him," Kelly said, reaching over and enveloping her little sister in a hug. Evan could see tears glistening in his big sister's eyes, too.

"Awww, they're all so sad you're away at Christmastime," the Sheriff sneered. "Isn't that touching. But I wonder why they miss such a miserable little grinch?"

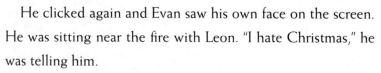

He clicked again and Evan saw his own face on the screen. He was sitting near the fire with Leon. "I hate Christmas," he was telling him.

The Sheriff cackled and hit the rewind button.

"I hate Christmas. I hate Christmas," Evan's image said.

"That's not what I meant," Evan shouted, not caring about the tears streaming down his cheeks. "What I hate about Christmas is exactly the kind of stuff that you're doing out there!" He gestured toward the door where Donner and Blitzen stood, their arms crossed in front of their chests.

"Out there?" the Sheriff asked in an oily voice. "Why, it's the very picture of Christmas out there."

Click.

Evan saw Merry and her family sitting in the portrait studio. The three girls were sitting in front of their parents, who stood behind them with proud expressions. The whole family was dressed in festive sweaters decorated with Christmas trees. Holly and Ivy grinned happily, their Miss Yuletide Carol sashes draped across their knees. As the photographer snapped, Merry's dad reached down and gently brushed a stray curl out of her face. Merry tipped her face up to beam at him.

The Sheriff froze the picture. "Now, there's a happy family at Christmas. My advice to you, my young friend, is that from now on, you be very, very careful about what kind of Humbug you spread. It's not right to question traditions, especially those we have perfectly good reasons for."

Spinning the remote like a pistol, he flipped it in the air, caught it, and slid it into a holster buckled around his waist. He grinned as he stepped in close to Evan, who trembled but didn't flinch away. "There are three more days left before all these frenzied shoppers go home, and I'm this close—" he pinched two fingers together and held them up in front of Evan's face"—to grossing over a million dollars this season. And *that* is what makes it a very merry Christmas for me."

The Sheriff snapped back upright, and in a move so quick Evan barely saw it happen, spun toward the screens, slipped the remote from the holster, and—*click*—images of the Complex reappeared. The Sheriff sat back down on his couch, fluffing the pillows behind him. He reached forward and picked up a gingerbread man from the table.

"I'm feeling the Christmas Spirit," he said magnanimously, waving the gingerbread man around. "And so I'm going to let you go this time. But I'll be watching you every minute, and I'd advise you not to make trouble. You've seen how you've already ruined Christmas for your family. You wouldn't want to ruin it for any others, now would you?"

"You could get rid of me for good," Evan pleaded. "You know who my parents are, where I live. Just tell me how to get home and I'll never bother you again."

"Well, actually, I can't do that, " the Sheriff said. "There's probably only one person who could."

"Tell me how to find them, then," Evan begged.

"I don't think so," the Sheriff said. " No one goes home until the Twelve Days of Christmas reaches a grand finale on the biggest sale day of the year. Besides, once the last clearance item is sold and we're packed up and on our way, you're not my problem anymore."

He bit the head off the gingerbread cookie and turned his attention back to the screens. "Now scram."

Donner and Blitzen stepped aside and opened the door. Scooping him up by each arm again, they deposited him out-side the gaily striped door and slammed it shut behind him.

EVAN STOOD OUTSIDE the Sheriff's office, trembling with anger. So there was a way for him to get home! The Sheriff had said there was one person who knew what the secret was. And Evan thought he had a pretty good idea himself. He thought back on Noel's suspicious behavior when they'd first met, how he wouldn't answer any of Evan's questions, how he had paced and muttered about "the right one," and "proceeding carefully." Yep, now that he thought about it, Evan was pretty sure Noel was hiding some big secret.

"Tricky little guy, sending me up here to get locked in with everyone else when he *knows* how I can get home. Well, now I'll be home soon enough. I just have to get out of here and find the little weasel."

Clenching and unclenching his fists, Evan forced himself to stroll slowly through the Complex, pretending to admire the shop windows. His mind was racing. He knew the Sheriff was watching but he just had to figure out how to get to Noel, and then he'd be gone for good.

Evan turned the corner and stopped abruptly. Merry and her family were headed right toward him. He ducked into the entrance of the Away from the Manger travel store and peeked around the edge of the doorway.

Merry's mom and sisters were striding along purposefully, swinging huge shopping bags, and pointing at different things in the storefronts they passed. But Merry was lagging behind, not paying any attention to the glittering displays in the windows.

Evan felt a pang as he watched her shuffle along. He wished he could bring her home and show her what it was like to stroll home along the snowy streets with their twinkling strands of Christmas lights. He thought she would like the feeling of coming home to a kitchen fragrant with the smells of Christmas baking and fresh evergreen. He wanted her to hear the clear voices of the neighbors as they stood out in front of the house and sang "Silver Bells."

He almost reached out and grabbed her arm as she walked past, but he didn't. Here he was trying to get home to his family, and at the same time he was thinking about taking someone away from theirs. It just wasn't right. But what the Sheriff had done wasn't right, either. This Complex was no place for Christmas.

Evan watched the back of Merry's head as she walked down the corridor.

"Bye," he whispered.

He closed his eyes and concentrated on recalling the diagram of the Complex. The aire vents were definitely the way to escape, if he could find another one. Suddenly he remembered: One of the arrows had pointed to a spot in the atrium near the living quarters.

Forcing himself to walk calmly, Evan strolled over to the area near the escalator. He ducked behind the moving stairs and into the elevator.

"Gotta work fast," he said to himself.

Evan let the elevator doors close, then pressed the "Stop" button. Hoisting himself up and bracing a foot on each of the handrails lining the elevator car, he stretched toward the panel in the ceiling. His fingertips barely brushed it. Desperate, he flung himself up into the air, punching his fist upward as he flew. The panel bumped up and shifted to the side.

Evan landed and quickly hit the express button for the top floor. As the elevator began to move, a disembodied voice came from the speaker near the control panel.

"Is everything all right? What's going on in there?"

Evan gupled and didn't answer.

As the elevator moved slowly upward, Evan climbed on the handrails and again jumped toward the ceiling. Catching the edge of the opening, he chinned himself up and wriggled through. As quietly as he could, he replaced the top panel.

Then he crouched down on the top of the elevator and hoped he had remembered the details from the map correctly. Glancing above him as the elevator ascended, Evan thought he could see a dim gray square above his head. The elevator slowed as it reached the top floor and Evan could see a large grate in the wall, nearly parallel to where he was crouched.

The elevator stopped. As the doors slid open, Evan heard someone yell, "Grab him!"

His heart began to race. The Police Navidad!

"He's not in here," another voice said.

"Then find him, you idiots." Evan heard the Sheriff's voice just underneath him.

There wasn't a moment to lose. Praying that this was his ticket out, Evan wrenched the grate free from the window. It fell on the top of the elevator with a loud metallic clang.

"He's up on top!"

"Move the panel!"

Using all his strength, Evan pushed the metal grate onto the top of the ceiling panel, which was just beginning to shift. He knew he had only moments. He hoisted himself up into the opening in the wall, and as he heard the scrape of the grate being pushed aside, hurled himself through.

Seven

THE BRACING COLD air of the outside world slapped
Evan in the face as he flew out through the aire vent and
landed with a thump on one of the giant drifts of snow banked
against the Complex. The momentum from his hasty escape
propelled him down the slope like a human snowboard, arms

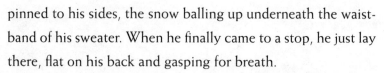

pinned to his sides, the snow balling up underneath the waist-band of his sweater. When he finally came to a stop, he just lay there, flat on his back and gasping for breath.

He was still moving his arms and legs experimentally, mak-ing sure he was all in one piece, when he was suddenly yanked to his feet.

"Let's go! We've got to get out of here, and fast." It was Noel, bundled against the cold in even more colorful and tat-tered layers than when Evan had first seen him.

Too stunned to protest, Evan let Noel lead the way back down to the village. He was vaguely aware of a commotion behind them as they ran, but Noel wouldn't let him slow down to look over his shoulder.

"This way, quickly," he urged, pulling Evan behind a row of evergreen shrubs in front of one of the houses. He ducked down, yanking Evan's arm. Evan squatted down next to him.

"You know how—" Evan started to say, before Noel clamped a hand over his mouth.

"Quiet," he whispered.

Evan froze as he saw a line of brightly colored red-and-green trousers ending in polished black boots marching past his line of vision. Footsteps echoed on the sidewalk as they passed the hedge where he and Noel were hidden. When the sound of footsteps had faded, Noel took his hand away from Evan's mouth.

"The Police Navidad," he said. "They must think you're headed for the castle."

"Why would I be headed for the castle?" Evan wanted to know, his curiosity overcoming his urge to throw Noel on the ground and sit on him until he revealed the secrets to leaving the snow globe.

"Why did you leave the Complex?"

Evan gritted his teeth. Noel's habit of answering a question with another question was infuriating.

"Why wouldn't I want to leave that place?" Evan braced himself for the inevitable question in reply.

"It's pretty horrible," Noel said sadly.

"Well, I'm out now," Evan said. "That's what matters. So if you could just tell me how to get back home, I'll forget that you were the one who sent me up there in the first place."

"I can't send you home," Noel said.

"What do you mean, you can't send me home?" Evan shouted in disbelief. "The Sheriff said there was one person who could do it. That person is you."

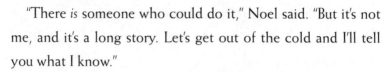

"There *is* someone who could do it," Noel said. "But it's not me, and it's a long story. Let's get out of the cold and I'll tell you what I know."

Evan realized he was shivering. He'd made his escape without a coat, and the snow that had slid up under his sweater was now dripping in icy streams down his back. He gratefully followed Noel into one of the little houses and allowed himself to be bundled up in piles of blankets.

Noel knelt down in front of the fireplace and pushed a button, and a cozy, glowing fire sprang to life. "Never thought I'd appreciate a gas fireplace," he said, rubbing his hands together cheerfully. "But the last thing we need is for the Police to see smoke."

Leaving Evan to huddle as close to the fire as he could, Noel left the room, returning shortly with two huge mugs full of steaming liquid.

Cradling his mug in two hands, Evan sniffed the steam rising from the drink. He could smell spices—cinnamon and nutmeg—and apples. It smelled delicious. He took a sip, feeling the warmth spreading to his cheeks and through his body.

"This is great," he said. "What is it?"

"Haven't you ever had wassail before?" Noel asked incredulously.

"So this is wassail," Evan said thoughtfully. "I always thought it was some kind of winter sport."

Noel burst out laughing. "Don't let the Sheriff hear that," he snorted. "Or he'll devise some sort of 'wassail tournament' for everyone up there to enter." He gestured in the direction of the Complex.

Evan laughed, too.

"Actually, wassail has been around since at least Saxon times, when people would wassail the apple trees in an orchard to ensure a good crop of apples for the coming year. *Wassail* comes from the words *wase haile*, which mean 'good health,'" Noel explained. "The people from the local community, and the people who owned the orchard, would pick a tree and pour cider on its roots, and place pieces of cake or toasted bread in its branches. Songs were sung and toasts made, all to the health of the tree."

"You mean, that Christmas carol is about pouring cider on trees?" Evan asked.

"Not exactly," Noel told him. "The custom evolved, as customs do, and soon bands of people called *wassails* went around with a special bowl, generally carved from apple wood. They would sing and offer good wishes for the coming year in exchange for food or drink. The kind of wassail we're drinking now was probably very much like the brew the singers were served by the townspeople."

"So this is a drink with a real history," Evan mused.

Noel nodded and they sat silently for a few minutes, savoring the warm brew.

"Noel, why do they let him do it?" Evan asked abruptly.

"Who? Do what?" Noel replied.

"The Sheriff. Why does everyone let him ruin their Christmas?"

Noel looked thoughtful. "I'm not sure they know it's being ruined. They've been spending Christmas at the Complex for so long now, that I think everyone just considers it a tradition."

"So they've always spent Christmas up there?" Evan asked.

"Not always," Noel said. "This village used to come alive at Christmas. There would be a traditional celebration at the castle, complete with a Christmas feast." His expression grew dreamy. "The halls would be decked with holly and ivy and evergreens. We would march out to the woods by moonlight and cut down the perfect tree, and bring it inside to be decorated with lights and ornaments. There would be games, and dancing, and beautiful music. The children would go to bed at night and dream of the treats they would find in their stockings the next morning. Even in the coldest, darkest winter, the castle glowed with light and hope on Christmas."

"So what happened?" Evan asked. "Why did everyone give that up for the kind of Christmas they have at the Complex?"

Noel sighed. "Well, I suppose people just got busier and busier, and gradually the real meaning of the season slipped away. Generations passed, each forgetting a little more about the ancient roots of the Christmas traditions. Once that happened, it was easy for someone like the Sheriff to come in and manufacture whatever kind of traditions they wanted to. People don't want meaningless celebrations, and the Sheriff knew that. He is clever, if evil. He made it seem as if his traditions existed for a reason. And gradually, people came to believe that things had always been that way."

"I guess people are more willing to hold on to ways of doing things if they think there's a reason," Evan said slowly, remembering that he'd thought of his family's traditions as "chores." "So then, why did you do all the stuff you did up at the castle?

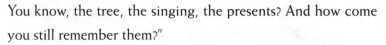
You know, the tree, the singing, the presents? And how come you still remember them?"

"I was a minstrel in the court of the castle," Noel said. "I sang the songs that kept the Christmas legends alive. And music is in your heart, as much as in your mind, so you never forget."

Evan understood perfectly. "Tell me about some of the traditions," he said. "All I know is that the first Christmas was the birthday of the baby Jesus."

"Ah, but many, many traditions of Christmas have been around for longer than that." Noel pulled a chair up close to Evan and sat down.

"In the oldest of times, the people of the northlands knew that the winter would be a hard season. The crops that they depended on for sustenance were gone and the earth was frozen under a blanket of white. It would have been easy to despair and to believe that spring would never return."

Evan nodded. He knew that feeling.

"But then they noticed that certain hardy plants—like holly, ivy, yew, and pine—remained bright spots of color in the barren landscape," Noel continued. "The people believed these plants possessed certain powers: the ability to chase off evil and shield their homes from demons. They brought these evergreen plants into their homes to protect them during the icy winters, and to remind them that spring would come and the earth would bloom again."

"So that's why we have Christmas trees," Evan said.

"Not exactly," Noel replied. "One snowy evening, in the sixteenth century, a German cleric named Martin Luther was out strolling and enjoying the beauty of the scenery. He became so transfixed by the sight of the fir trees dressed in snow, the bright stars in the clear night sky seeming to rest twinkling on their outstretched branches, that when he returned home, he wanted to re-create the effect for his family. He brought a small evergreen tree into his home and placed candles among its branches."

"That doesn't sound too safe," Evan said.

"Well, it wasn't exactly," Noel admitted. "In 1882, Edward Johnson, who was an associate of Thomas Edison's—"

"The guy who invented the lightbulb?"

"The same guy," Noel said. "Anyway, Mr. Johnson handwired small bulbs and wound them around a Christmas tree. No one really paid much attention until three years later, when President Grover Cleveland commissioned a White House Christmas tree lighted with 'Edison Bulbs.' Even though

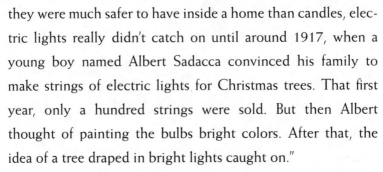

they were much safer to have inside a home than candles, electric lights really didn't catch on until around 1917, when a young boy named Albert Sadacca convinced his family to make strings of electric lights for Christmas trees. That first year, only a hundred strings were sold. But then Albert thought of painting the bulbs bright colors. After that, the idea of a tree draped in bright lights caught on."

Evan was impressed that someone not much older than he was had been responsible for a tradition that still existed.

"What about mistletoe?" Evan couldn't believe that there was a good reason for kissing under a plant.

"Mistletoe, eh?" Noel grinned. "Now there's a tradition that's truly been passed down through the centuries. Hundreds of years before the birth of Christ, the Druids used mistletoe to celebrate the coming of winter. They believed the plant had special healing powers and would use it to decorate their homes. The Scandinavians also thought of mistletoe as a plant of peace and harmony. They associated it with their goddess of love, Frigga."

"The goddess of *love*?" Evan asked, a sinking feeling in his stomach.

"Hence, the kissing traditions," Noel said, laughing as Evan squinched up his face in disgust.

Noel went on, explaining many other Christmas legends. He told Evan how the star on the top of the Christmas tree represented the star that was bright in the sky over the stable where the baby Jesus lay. The star had served as a beacon to guide the Wise Men to the child so they could honor him with gifts.

He also told the story of Saint Nicholas, a good and generous man, whose acts of kindness and charity were carried on today by the person Evan called Santa Claus, a jolly and generous soul who was known by different names to children all around the world.

And he told Evan how the earliest Christmas songs were chants and hymns, and how many simple folk used songs to commemorate the feelings of Christmas, and how those songs were passed down through time to become some of the Christmas carols we sing today.

Noel looked out the window at the darkened streets of the town. "We used to carol through these very streets, like the waits of old."

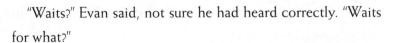

"Waits?" Evan said, not sure he had heard correctly. "Waits for what?"

" 'Waits' is a seventeenth-century word that means 'watchmen,' " Noel explained. "They would patrol the streets of the old walled cities at night, keeping guard against fire and singing out the hours of the night. Legend has it that during the Christmas season, they would include some carols for people as they made their rounds. Today, when people go out caroling in the streets, they're reliving that tradition."

As Noel talked, Evan began to understand how the ways of celebrating Christmas connected ancient and modern times. He realized that the traditions his family celebrated, like his father's insistence on cutting down a tree, or his mother's wreaths of holly and evergreen, were centuries old. Suddenly the "Christmas chores" he had resented took on an importance that defined the season.

"I totally get it," Evan said, when Noel paused. "For centuries, families have been gathering together to bring light and love and laughter into a dark time of year. And all of these things we do, they're just symbols to help us remember what Christmas is really about—a celebration of hope and faith. About believing that good exists in the world, and that love can sustain us through the darkest of winter days until spring brings rebirth."

Noel nodded. "Traditions of Christmas, and all traditions, for that matter, are the glue that bind all mankind together. It is the stuff of souls—what makes man different from all other living things. Honoring tradition is part of what changes the waking body from an empty shell to a living, feeling being."

"I can feel it," Evan agreed. "Now that you've told me these stories, I can really feel what Christmas is about."

"We are all connected," Noel told him. "And traditions and storytelling connect us to our past, just as they project us into our future."

"So you can see why I have to get back home to my family in time for Christmas," Evan said, his voice breaking. "You see why I can't stay here."

"I'd help you if I could," Noel told him, his expression changing to one of deep sadness. "But I'm afraid that this isn't the only place that will be missing Christmas this year." He shook his head sadly. "I don't think there will be Christmas *anywhere* this year."

EVAN SAT stunned. No Christmas? Impossible. When he became lost in the storm, Christmas was just two days away; everyone was preparing for it. Of course Christmas was going to come.

"Why do you say that?" he demanded. "What do you know?"

Noel dropped his head into his hands. His shoulders slumped and he looked so tiny and tired that Evan got up and went over to put a comforting hand on his shoulder.

Noel looked up and tried to smile, but Evan could see tears brimming in his eyes. Taking a deep breath, Noel composed himself.

"For longer than you can imagine, the Christmas Spirit has been kept alive in that castle on the hill. The master of the castle would joyously begin the celebration here in the village, then, on Christmas Eve, he'd leave and spread the spirit of Christmas throughout the land."

Evan's eyes grew wide. Was Noel saying what he thought he was saying?

"But as the Sheriff began to gain a hold over the minds of the townsfolk, the master of the castle began to grow dispirited. At first when everyone left for the Complex, he would continue to decorate the castle halls and prepare the Christmas Feast. Each year, for more years than I can count, he did this, saying: 'If only one person comes to the castle, if only one person listens to their heart and believes, then Christmas shall live in this land.' But no one came. And gradually he stopped preparing for Christmas, and the castle fell into ruin." Noel shook his head sadly.

"Oh, he'd still go out on Christmas Eve to spread the joy of the season in other lands, but each time he came home, he was more and more disheartened. He said it was a losing battle. He saw the same changes that happened here, happening in other towns and villages. More and more, people were forgetting the old ways, not bothering to hand down the traditions that have connected us all through the ages.

"When he came back from his travels last year, he told me he would not go out again. And now he's hidden himself away in the castle keep and won't see anyone. Not even me." Noel wiped at the tears that were now running down his cheeks. "He's the only person who could have helped you to get home, but you'll never get him to talk to you."

"And the master of the castle." Evan hardly dared to ask the question. "What is his name?"

"Kringle," Noel said, sniffling.

"*What* did you say?"

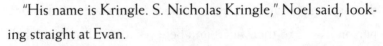

"His name is Kringle. S. Nicholas Kringle," Noel said, looking straight at Evan.

Evan's heart suddenly filled with hope. "I can get him to see me," he exclaimed. "I know I can. And maybe, just maybe, I can get you your Christmas back. But I've got to hurry." He jumped to his feet and threw off the blankets around his shoulders.

"Where are you going?" Noel asked. "I told you, it won't do any good to go up to the castle."

"I believe you," Evan said. "But I'm not going to the castle yet. I have to go back to the Complex first. There's someone there who can help us."

Eight

EVAN SKIRTED the edges of the Complex, his breath coming in frosty bursts. What if he got caught? Or worse, what if he couldn't get in at all? The night was biting cold, and although Noel had given him one of his tattered coats, Evan shivered incessantly.

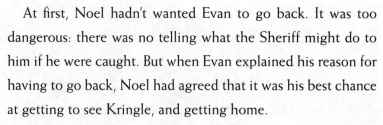

At first, Noel hadn't wanted Evan to go back. It was too dangerous: there was no telling what the Sheriff might do to him if he were caught. But when Evan explained his reason for having to go back, Noel had agreed that it was his best chance at getting to see Kringle, and getting home.

Noel had given Evan some of his clothing and pulled his odd tasseled cap off his head and settled it down around Evan's ears. "If they think it's me lurking around out there, they'll be less inclined to bother coming out," he'd explained. "They pretty much think I'm crazy but harmless. The worst they'd do is bring out the snow cannons to run me off."

Evan didn't even want to know what the snow cannons were; he couldn't afford to lose his nerve.

Noel had walked him outside the house. "Be careful, my friend." He broke a tiny branch off a small evergreen standing near the porch. "Take this with you. For hope."

Evan had tucked the branch into his pocket, and with a wave and what he hoped was a brave smile, loped off toward the Complex.

And so, sometime later under the moonless midnight sky, Evan found himself circling around the foreboding cement walls of the Complex, searching for a way back in. There was no way he could climb back up to the aire vents, and if he tried the front door again he'd surely be caught.

"C'mon," Evan muttered, blowing on his fingers to keep them warm. "There's got to be another way into this place."

He rounded another corner and almost ran smack into a huge, long container that looked kind of like a railroad car. He crept closer to explore. At one end of the container was a giant label: INVENTORY FOR GIANT SELLOUT. DO NOT OPEN UNTIL DECEMBER 24.

Just then he heard the *swooshing* sound of a door opening. There was no time to think. There was a handle next to the label, and he grabbed it and gave a mighty tug. To his great relief, the container wrenched open a crack.

Evan ducked inside, crouched down behind a stack of crates, and listened intently.

"All right, let's get this merchandise inside," a deep voice said.

"And let's get it on the shelves tonight, people." Evan nearly stopped breathing when he heard the Sheriff's snarling voice.

There was a scraping sound and the clanking of metal, and then Evan felt the container begin to move.

"Sure, easy for him to say," someone grunted. "He's probably going back to sack out and dream of a green Christmas."

Evan realized they were pulling the container into the Complex. He slipped out of the clothes Noel had lent him and began to paw through some of the crates, hoping to find a disguise. It wasn't easy in the dark, but Evan grabbed what felt like a sweater and something else that felt like a baseball cap with antlers. He opened another crate, and found that it was full of plush animals.

"Okay, let's open her up and get to work," a high, squeaky voice said.

Evan dived in among the animals, pulled the hat on, crossed his fingers and hoped.

He could hear the sounds of crates being unloaded. Footsteps drew closer and he felt himself being lifted into the air. The crate rose, then fell abruptly.

"Geez, what's in here? I'm gonna put my back out." The squeaky voice was right above Evan's head, outside the crate.

Evan felt the crate settle down on the floor. Not daring to breathe, he crouched down among the fuzzy creatures. He heard the flaps open, then the same voice.

"How could stuffed animals weigh so much?"

"Hey, Ed, we gotta get moving here; stop playing with the toys," A deeper voice called from across the room.

"All right, Dave, all right. Just let me get this thing closed up again. I'm gonna have to leave it here until I can get the forklift. I swear, I never knew stuffed animals could be so heavy."

Evan felt a hand press down on top of his head, and he sank lower until the reindeer hat was pressed down level with the rest of his furry companions. He let out his breath as the carton was closed back up. Then he heard the footsteps move away. He was eager to get out of the carton and into the Complex, but he knew he had to be cautious.

There was more thumping and scraping as the rest of the crates were unloaded, and soon Evan got his chance.

"Okay, I'm taking my break," Ed announced.

"The Sheriff is going to be furious if we don't get this stuff around to the stores," Dave said.

"The union's going to be furious if they find out I didn't get my break," Ed pointed out. "Let's go down to the all-night coffee shop and get us a cup of joe."

"Yeah, all right," Dave said. "But we gotta finish unloading tonight. The Sheriff wants lots of fresh inventory on the shelves."

Evan waited until he couldn't hear their footsteps anymore. And then he waited a few minutes longer.

"Well, I guess it's now or never," he told the stuffed bear that had been staring at him nose to nose since he'd dived inside the crate.

Evan climbed out and pulled on the bright red sweater he had grabbed, noting that it was decorated with images of flying reindeer. Feeling sort of pleased with himself for being able to pick out a coordinating outfit in the dark, he decided to keep the cap, despite the wacky antlers. They'd be looking for him anyway; maybe hiding in plain sight was best.

The halls of the Complex, which usually looked like the midway at a carnival, were oddly quiet. There were no shoppers rushing from store to store, although the stores all had lights on and Evan could see the employees frantically restocking the shelves. Pulling his reindeer cap further down on his head and clutching a shopping bag in each hand, he hoped he looked like a late shopper making his way back to his condo.

As he reached the end of the shops, Evan glanced around. Good, still no sign of the Police Navidad. He began to jog down the hallway that led to the atrium. He planned to hide beneath the branches of the huge Christmas tree and wait until morning. Then he was going to go and see Merry.

The tree was so big that once he had removed his antlers, Evan only had to crouch down a little to duck under the lowest of its spreading branches. Once underneath, he quickly clambered up onto a low branch and, resting his back against the wide trunk, settled in to wait for morning.

He was staring up at the twinkling lights strung through the branches above him and feeling his eyelids grow heavy, when he heard a rustling just above him.

"Who's there?" he whispered.

The rustling grew closer, then stopped.

"I thought you might come back," a voice said softly in his ear.

Evan started, losing his balance on the branch. Frantically hooking his legs around the branch, he ended up hanging on by his arms and legs, like a giant three-toed sloth.

Merry slipped around from the other side of the tree trunk, her hand clamped over her mouth, barely stifling her giggles.

"Geez," Evan said, righting himself on the branch. "You shouldn't sneak up on people like that."

"Look who's talking about sneaking," Merry said pointedly. "I thought you were just going to walk around and check things out. Why didn't you tell me you were going to break out of the Complex?"

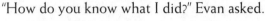

"How do you know what I did?" Evan asked.

"Everybody knows," she said. "You've been officially identified as a Humbug. The Police have put out bulletins offering a free shopping spree to the person who captures you. I had to promise Holly and Ivy my shopping allowance for the rest of The Big Sellout if they wouldn't turn you in."

"Thanks," he mumbled.

"You should have stayed away, Evan," Merry continued seriously. "I don't know what the Sheriff will do if he catches you. When I heard you broke out, and then you didn't meet me back here like we had agreed, I thought you went home without saying good-bye. So where were you, and why did you come back?"

"I had to come back," Evan said simply. "I need your help."

"My help? Doing what?"

"I can't get home without your help. But if everything goes like I hope it does, I'll get home, and you'll never have to worry about the Sheriff again." Evan smiled confidently and waited for Merry to ask what she should do.

"Don't be crazy," she said. "I can't help you to get home. You just need to hide until the Twelve Days are over. Then you can go home when everyone else does."

"I have to be home for Christmas," Evan said urgently, his confidence fading. "You don't understand, I know. But I can explain, I really can."

Merry stood up, hooking her arms on the tree branch above her for balance. She tipped her head back and stared toward the top of the tree, far overhead. When she looked back down at him, her expression was searching.

"What do you need me to do?" she asked.

"I need you to come with me to meet someone," Evan said carefully.

"Someone in the Complex?"

"No, on the outside."

Merry shook her head. "No way." She began climbing down from the tree. "I can't take the chance of being caught. My dad, it would kill him. I'd be an outcast, or worse."

"Please, Merry," Evan begged.

She reached the bottom of the tree. "I'm sorry, Evan," she said. "Good luck." She began to walk toward the escalator.

"The person we need to see is the guy from the poster— your great-great grandfather," Evan said softly to her back.

Merry stopped walking, but didn't turn around.

"He lives in the castle," Evan continued, talking fast. "He

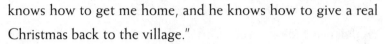

knows how to get me home, and he knows how to give a real Christmas back to the village."

Merry turned around and started back toward the tree. Evan was surprised to see that she looked furious.

"All you talk about is getting Christmas back," she stormed as she marched toward him. "Like we don't have a Christmas of our own. Like you've got the only *real* Christmas, with all your stupid traditions." She stared up to where he was perched on the branch.

"Every time you mention Christmas, it's like your way is so much better: dragging trees and evergreens into your house where they all shed their needles on the carpet, and standing around under some stupid plant kissing, and people all running around in the streets singing in loud voices and keeping everyone awake."

Evan swung down from the branch and faced her eye to eye. He opened his mouth to protest, but Merry held her hand up.

"At least our traditions have meanings. They've been passed down from generation to generation. I've always celebrated Christmas this way, and it's not up to you to say it's not right." She stopped to draw a breath.

"Well actually, I *can* tell you why we have indoor Christmas trees, but that's beside the point right now." Evan took a deep breath. "Merry, if you'll answer one question for me—honestly—then I won't bug you anymore. You can forget I ever even asked."

"Fine," Merry said, her jaw still clenched.

Evan chose his words carefully. "How does Christmas make you feel?"

"Feel?"

"Yes, feel. When you think about The Big Sellout, are you full of hope and anticipation? Do you find joy in searching out just the right pair of gold-plated nose hair trimmers for your dad? Do you like following your sisters around all day while they shop? If it could be different, somehow, wouldn't you want it to be?"

Merry's face softened. "It's supposed to be a special time," she said quietly. "But we get so busy that the whole family is hardly ever all together."

Evan reached for her hand. "Come here." He pulled her back under the branches of the tree. Reaching into his pocket, he pulled out the small fir branch and bent it, releasing the fragrance of sap and pine. He handed it to her.

"Now look up at the lights and pretend they're stars. And don't talk, just listen."

Evan closed his eyes and began to sing.

> Silent night, Holy night.
> All is calm. All is bright.

As he sang, he pictured his family gathered around the fire, Elyse with her arms around his dad's neck, her eyes heavy with sleep as Kelly and his mother hung the stockings in order: Mom, Dad, Kelly, Evan, Elyse. He imagined his mother going around the room, turning off the lights until the family sat together on the couch, bathed in firelight, quiet and content. He sang like they had sung every Christmas Eve since he could remember.

> Sleep in heavenly peace.
> Sleep in heavenly peace.

When he opened his eyes, he half expected to see the worn brown leather of his living room couch. Instead he saw Merry's eyes, green and gold and bright with tears.

"Christmas isn't out there," he said, gesturing toward the Complex. He took her hand and laid it on his heart. "Christmas is in here."

Merry's eyes were shining like stars. "I'll help," she whispered.

Nine

EVAN CROUCHED down behind one of the topiary snowmen guarding the steel doors at the entrance to the hallway leading to the main door of the Complex. Though it was just past dawn on the morning of Christmas Eve, the Complex was already humming with activity.

"THE EARLY BIRD CATCHES THE WARM," blared the loudspeakers. "FIRST FIFTY PEOPLE TO VISIT RUDY'S RUSSIAN FOUL WEATHER SHOP WILL RECEIVE COUPONS FOR TEN PERCENT OFF ON THE PURCHASE OF A FLANNEL-LINED UMBRELLA. REMEMBER FOLKS, RUDOLPH THE RED KNOWS RAIN GEAR."

A wave of people surged toward the door of the shop, shouting and waving their hands.

Evan had been crouching for so long that his knees were beginning to ache when Merry finally showed up. Her face was flushed and she was slightly out of breath. She ducked behind the snowman on the other side of the doorway.

"What took you so long?" he asked.

"I ran almost all the way here," she panted. "It took forever to get out of the house. My dad was searching all over for his master key to the Complex. He made everyone in the family help and I thought he'd never leave. But there's a big meeting with the Sheriff and the rest of the Force this morning, so he finally had to go."

"Did he ever find the key?" Evan asked.

Merry held up something that looked like a remote control for a garage door.

"Nope," she grinned. "We'd better hurry, though, before the Police get out of their meeting."

"All right," Evan said. "On 'three' we make a break for it. One. Two. Three."

Evan reached up and pushed the green button on the wall, hidden from view behind the snowman's top hat. The steel doors slid silently open.

Darting out from behind the snowmen, Evan and Merry ran full tilt down the hallway, screeching to a halt as a blank-looking wall loomed up in front of them.

"Are you sure this is right?" Merry asked. "I don't see a door anywhere."

"This is definitely where I came in the first time," Evan said. "Just watch."

He took the device from her hand, pointed it at the wall, and pushed the red button. With a soft *swoosh* the wall slid back, revealing a perfect winter wonderland on the other side.

Evan and Merry were transfixed. The sun was just rising in the eastern sky. The glowing orb hung low, bathing the freshly fallen snow in a golden glow. Icicles hanging from tree branches caught the morning rays and reflected them back, sparkling like fiery diamonds. The whole world looked ablaze against the backdrop of a perfect, clear blue sky.

"It's so beautiful," Merry gasped.

"So peaceful," Evan murmured.

They stepped through the opening and Evan turned, aiming the device at the door to close it.

Suddenly the calm morning air was shattered by the sound of clanging alarms. Horns blared, whistles shrilled, and a voice thundered, "Warning. Warning. Security has been breached. Code Red. Code Red."

Grabbing Merry's hand, Evan began running down the hill toward the village.

"Prepare the cannons," the loudspeakers boomed.

Evan heard a whizzing sound near his ear, then felt a thump between his shoulder blades. He pitched forward into the snow. Rolling over onto his side, he saw the air was filled with snowballs.

"Snow cannons," Merry said, dropping to her knees to avoid the hard-packed spheres hurtling over her head.

They moved as fast as they could on all fours, until they were out of range of the hard, white missiles. Then they got to their feet and started to run again. The snow was deep—to their knees in some spots, deeper in others. Evan glanced over his shoulder, squinting against the bright sun in his eyes. He could see the brightly colored uniforms of the Police Navidad as they milled about at the entrance to the Complex.

"Hurry, Merry," he urged.

"They're coming after us!" she said, looking back. Evan could hear the panic in her voice.

The Police were shooting down the hill, riding on wooden sleds that flew smoothly over the drifts of snow.

"Flexible Flyers," Evan said in dismay.

It was the same kind of sled he used in the ravine behind his house, and he knew just how fast they were. The Police were closer now; he could hear their voices calling out over the frozen ground.

"Halt. We command that you surrender."

Evan and Merry finally reached the edge of the village. Grateful for the rough footing of blacktop that lay just under the snow dusting the roads, they sped toward the castle.

Behind them, they could hear the Police Navidad jumping off their sleds. Their thick-soled boots pounded the pavement. Someone barked orders. "All right, everyone, spread out. They can't hide from us for long."

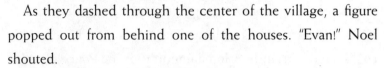

As they dashed through the center of the village, a figure popped out from behind one of the houses. "Evan!" Noel shouted.

"Noel, they're right behind us," Evan said, breathing so hard he could hardly talk. His blood was pounding in his ears and his heart was racing. He didn't know if he could walk, never mind run, another step.

There was a loud buzzing sound at the end of the street, and Noel, Merry, and Evan ducked behind a large woodpile. Peeking out, they saw the Sheriff, wrapped in a huge white fur coat, zooming down the street on a glistening black snowmobile. He stopped at the end of the road and they could hear his furious bellow.

"If those two kids are not found, it'll be the end of you, Kringle. Mark my words, you will pay and pay dearly."

"Dad," Merry whispered sadly.

"Now get these men of yours in line and GET ME THOSE BRATS." The Sheriff's words echoed through the empty streets and bounced off the deserted buildings.

"I've got an idea," Noel whispered. "I'm going to distract them, and then you two take off. Good luck."

Before Evan or Merry could protest, Noel jumped out from behind the woodpile. He grabbed a garden hose that was lying next to the woodpile and, checking that it was still connected, he turned the spigot and ran out toward the street, trailing drops of water behind him.

"Hey guys!" he shouted, jumping up and down in the middle of the street to get the Police's attention. "Over here."

The Sheriff gunned his snowmobile and tore down the street, aiming right for Noel like an angry bull bearing down on a bullfighter. Noel stood his ground, waving the spraying water like a red cape. The Police were running as hard as they could, struggling to keep up with the Sheriff's sleek machine.

"Now!" Noel yelled over his shoulder to Evan and Merry, who sprinted from the woodpile like rabbits fleeing the hounds.

Behind them, they heard the Sheriff's screams and Noel's ringing laughter. Evan couldn't resist looking back. The water from the hose had covered the street in front of Noel with a thin layer of ice. The Sheriff had hit the icy edge, and his snowmobile was spinning out of control. The Police didn't see what was happening until it was too late. As they stepped onto the ice and tried to slide to a stop, the snowmobile careened

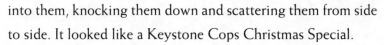

into them, knocking them down and scattering them from side to side. It looked like a Keystone Cops Christmas Special.

Evan gave Noel a wave of thanks, and he and Merry were soon at the rocky outcropping below the castle. They carefully picked their way up, finding footholds among the snow-covered rocks. As they drew closer to the castle, Evan could see that the drawbridge was down.

"This is it," he said, as they paused at the edge of the drawbridge.

Merry nodded. She looked a little frightened.

"It's all going to work out," Evan said reassuringly, walking slowly across the drawbridge toward the huge doorway.

"Merry!"

They both wheeled in the direction of the voice.

Merry's father stood among the rocks just below the drawbridge. His gold uniform was wet and muddy in spots and his hat had been knocked off, revealing red hair with curls as unruly as Merry's.

"You need to come home, Merry," he said, holding a hand out in her direction.

Merry hesitated.

"I know what you're looking for, honey," her dad said, edging closer to the drawbridge. "But it doesn't exist. You're chasing something no one believes in anymore."

Evan felt a rumbling beneath his feet, and the drawbridge began to rise slowly. Merry lost her balance and slipped to her knees. Clinging to the edge of the drawbridge as it tipped upward, she looked down at her father.

"Have faith, Daddy," Merry called out. "*I* believe. And I'll be back soon with proof!" She let go of the drawbridge and slid down the inclined plank, landing in the doorway next to Evan with a thump.

THE CASTLE WAS cold and dark, the large stones underfoot slick with frost. Evan and Merry moved slowly through the rooms, peering up at the magnificently arched ceiling and massive stone staircases.

"Noel said that the master of the castle had locked himself in the keep," Evan said.

"What's a keep?" Merry wanted to know.

"It's the safest and most protected part of the castle," Evan said. "Like a castle within a castle."

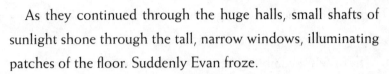
As they continued through the huge halls, small shafts of sunlight shone through the tall, narrow windows, illuminating patches of the floor. Suddenly Evan froze.

"Listen," he said. "Do you hear that?"

The heavy silence of the castle closed in around them.

Then he heard the noise again: Shuffling footsteps echoed softly at the end of one of the long hallways. It sounded as if someone was slowly going up the stairs.

Gesturing for Merry to stay slightly behind him, Evan moved quietly down the hall until he arrived at an enormous metal door. The shuffling noises sounded closer now. Evan reached up and grabbed the huge metal ring in the center of the door, and pulled with all his might. The door didn't budge.

He felt Merry's arms around his waist, and he leaned back to tug at the door again as Merry pulled, too. The door slowly and silently cracked open. Evan wriggled through with Merry close behind.

They were in a huge circular tower room. The room was totally empty, except for a tall pine tree that was leaning against the wall, as if forgotten. A curving staircase ran along the walls to a floor above and to one below. Overhead, they heard the slow shuffle of footsteps.

"I'm going up," Evan whispered.

"I'm going, too," Merry said.

They tiptoed their way up the wide stone staircase.

The stairs ended in another round tower room, this one lined with shelves that held fat leather ledgers. A large wooden writing desk, with an old-fashioned quill pen and a scroll of paper spilling to the floor, sat in the middle of the room. Tall, narrow windows let the morning sun into the room and illuminated the maps and charts hanging on the walls. A huge trunk was propped open, and bright red robes spilled over the edges.

And then Evan saw him. A tall, thin man with ramrod straight posture stood at one of the windows overlooking the village below, his back to the room. He was dressed in a shabby old plaid bathrobe and was wearing leather slippers lined with fur.

"Excuse me." Evan cleared his throat. "Excuse me, Mr. Kringle?"

The man at the window turned around, and Evan saw he had a long white beard and a very kind face. "I've been expecting you, Evan."

Evan's mouth dropped open. "How did you know my name?"

"I have a list," the man said vaguely, gesturing toward his desk, then turning back to the window. "Have you come from down there?"

"Well, yes. But—no," Evan stammered, still trying to get his bearings.

"I suppose it really doesn't matter," the man said wearily, pulling his robe around him more tightly.

"Noel sent me," Evan blurted out.

The man turned around again. "He's a dreamer, Noel is," the man said softly. "I suppose he sent you up here to try to change my mind."

"Is it true then, what Noel says? Are you canceling Christmas?" Evan asked in dismay.

"It's true. I haven't got the heart for it anymore. It's too much for one soul to carry on."

"Oh, please," Evan begged. "Don't do that. I want to have Christmas."

"Without all the *chores*?" The man's piercing blue eyes seemed to look straight into Evan's heart.

"I'm different, now," Evan protested. "I really understand. I do. I really believe in the spirit of Christmas."

"Yes, yes, very nice of you to say so," the man said bitterly. "But I'm afraid it's just too little, too late."

Evan was speechless, stunned by what he was hearing. No Christmas?

"I believe, too." Merry stepped out of the shadows of the stairs and stood next to Evan. "I believe, and I have hope." She held out the sprig of evergreen Evan had given her.

Evan watched the man's eyes light up as he took it from her hand.

"And I'm your great-great granddaughter, so I *know* I have the Christmas Spirit in me. And if you don't want to do it this year, then tell me how, and I will." Merry crossed her arms in front of her chest and lifted her chin.

The old man burst out laughing. His laughter rang off the walls and echoed through the chamber, pealing like bells. When he finally composed himself, he walked over to Merry and gently cupped his hand under her chin.

"Well, it's a few more 'greats' than just two," he said to her. "But I can see that the Christmas Spirit does burn bright within you." His expression turned somber. "We have so much work to do, though, and it's so late. I don't know if it can all be done."

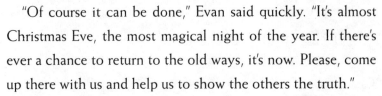

"Of course it can be done," Evan said quickly. "It's almost Christmas Eve, the most magical night of the year. If there's ever a chance to return to the old ways, it's now. Please, come up there with us and help us to show the others the truth."

"I've put my whole family in danger," Merry said urgently. "My dad could lose his job because of me." She paused. "Actually, I guess I hope he does. But I want my family to have the kind of Christmas that matters. And you're the only one who can help us. So please . . ."

The man sighed and ran his fingers through his unkempt hair. "The innocence of children," he murmured to himself. "Will it be enough?"

Evan and Merry held their breath and waited.

After a long silence, the man seemed to arrive at a decision. Crossing over to the trunk, he pulled out a long, red cloak.

"All right," he said. "I'll go with you. But I must warn you: It won't be easy. Any Christmas magic I may have left is bound to be rusty. And honestly, kids, I don't have any sort of a plan."

Ten

THE SUN WAS sinking close to the horizon as Evan, Merry, and the mysterious man called Kringle headed down toward the Complex. Evan urged the others to move quickly, feeling a sense of urgency. Several hours had passed since he

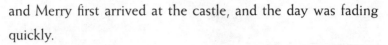

and Merry first arrived at the castle, and the day was fading quickly.

Once Kringle had agreed to return to the Complex with them, Evan had explained the origins of Christmas traditions to Merry, while Kringle changed into long, flowing robes of red and gold and covered them with a long, hooded cloak trimmed in white fur. As Merry and Evan shivered in the setting sun, he gestured for them to wrap themselves in the warm folds of his cloak.

"So, who are you really?" Evan asked the man as they walked.

"I'm different things to different people," he replied.

"Yeah, but your last name, Kringle . . ." Evan persisted. "And Noel said your first name was S. Nicholas—like *Saint Nicholas?*"

"It's true that those are my names," he said simply.

"Well, do you have magic powers?" Merry asked bluntly.

"I am the keeper of the magic of Christmas," he said.

"Cool!" Evan was excited. "You're like a wizard. That is so cool. So—what kind of magic can you do?"

"I'm afraid my magic is weak now," Kringle admitted. "It is fueled by the Christmas Spirit, which has been woefully lacking over the last few years."

"So you can't just zap the Sheriff?" Evan asked hopefully.

Kringle shook his head.

Evan peered around at Merry. "Got any ideas yet?"

She shook her head.

Evan's heart began to race as the Complex loomed up in front of them. He had to admit he was afraid to return. He'd convinced the Police Captain's daughter to run away from home, and the Sheriff would have no mercy. *No, there is no way this is going to be easy.*

"You sure you don't just want to come home with me and have Christmas with my family?" Evan asked Merry hopefully.

Merry gave him a look that clearly implied he was nuts. "Christmas is about family," she said adamantly.

"Well, here we are," Evan said, trying to sound optimistic as the three arrived in front of the blank wall that was the main door to the Complex. "Okay, Merry, you do the honors with the opener."

Merry gasped. "The opener?" She patted her pockets frantically. "I don't have it. I thought you had it."

Evan checked his pockets. "I don't have it. It must have dropped when we were escaping."

Merry looked as if she was about to cry. "They won't let us in," she said. "They'd rather see us freeze out here than open the door."

As she spoke, the door slid open. Evan wheeled around to see Kringle, his finger extended, pointed at the door.

"Guess you've got a little magic left, huh?" he said with a wide grin.

Kringle gave a small shrug. "I hope it's enough," he said.

Evan and Merry stepped through the doorway and into the Complex. A rush of warm air greeted them and Evan gratefully stomped his freezing feet, trying to get some feeling back in his toes. "It's not like we have to be quiet," he said in response to Merry's arched eyebrow. "I mean, we're not sneaking in this time, are we?"

Kringle lagged behind as Merry and Evan made their way down the hall. "Go on ahead," he called out. "I need to rest for a minute."

"So what's the plan?" Evan asked as they reached the end of the corridor and prepared to step out into the Complex.

"I want to find my dad, to explain," Merry said.

Evan nodded, and they stepped through the doorway guarded by the topiary snowmen.

"Gotcha, you rotten little Humbugs!"

The Police swooped down on Merry and Evan, snatching them up by the arms and dragging them over to a very peeved-looking Sheriff.

"Shouldn't have much trouble finding your dad," Evan muttered out of the side of his mouth.

The Sheriff stepped forward. "Well, well, well. Look what's crawled back for Christmas," he sneered. "Decided you couldn't stand the thought of a December twenty-fifth without presents? Well, I've got a special one for you."

He nodded and Captain Kringle stepped up in front of Evan and Merry, dragging Noel along.

"Let me go, you big oaf." Noel kicked and struggled until he saw Merry and Evan. "Hey, Evan," he said brightly. "Did you find him?"

Evan nodded. "Yeah, he's right behind us." He craned his head around, but there was no one in the doorway.

"Secure the exit corridor," the Sheriff barked, and three of the Police set off at a brisk trot toward the door.

"Now, what to do with you three Humbugs . . ." the Sheriff said thoughtfully, tapping a huge candy cane rhythmically against his open palm. "I need to make a proper example of you."

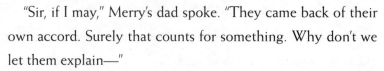

"Sir, if I may," Merry's dad spoke. "They came back of their own accord. Surely that counts for something. Why don't we let them explain—"

"Don't go soft on me, Kringle," the Sheriff cut him off. "We can't have these troublemakers running around, questioning The Big Sellout, blabbering nonsense about *real* Christmases." He shook his head sadly. "Your own daughter, too."

A crowd was beginning to gather around the Sheriff and his captives.

"There's no one in the exit tunnel, Sheriff," Officer Donner announced loudly as they returned.

An excited buzz went through the crowd. Had someone left the Complex? Before the end of The Big Sellout? Was there an intruder?

The Sheriff raised his hands appeasingly. "Quiet down, folks, quiet down. Nothing's going on here. We're just suppressing a few Humbugs. Protecting you from radical fringe elements."

He turned to an officer standing near him and whispered, "Get over to the sales office and have them announce a red-and green-light special. Pronto!"

The officer sprinted off.

The Sheriff turned back to the crowd, which had grown even bigger. "I see lots of empty hands out there, people. Shouldn't you all be getting in some last-minute shopping? While you stand here gawking, someone else could be buying the very item you need. I promise you, there's nothing interesting going on here."

The crowd began to mill around, shifting restlessly to gaze out at the shops lining the main hall.

Evan felt Officer Blitzen's grip on his arm relax, and like lightning, he jumped up on a display of gaily wrapped Christmas boxes. "There *is* something interesting going on here, and the Sheriff doesn't want you to know about it!" he shouted to the crowd.

Merry wriggled free from Officer Dasher to join him.

"GET THEM DOWN!" the Sheriff roared.

The commotion attracted even more shoppers.

Merry looked right at her father. "Dad, listen to me. There's much more to Christmas than all this." She gestured out toward the shops. "I didn't believe it at first, either. But now I do."

Merry jumped down from the boxes and ran over to her

dad. Captain Kringle released Noel, and held out his hand to his daughter. "All right, honey. I can see you've been influenced by the friends you're hanging around with, and I'm sure the Sheriff can forgive a lapse in judgment. Just say you'll come home with me and we'll work this all out. I'll get you something really special," he promised.

"Don't you see, Dad? Christmas isn't about getting. It's about giving," Merry said.

"The child is right," a voice from within the crowd said.

As Captain Kringle watched, an astonished look on his face, a tall, distinguished man in flowing red and gold robes made his way toward Merry and her father.

When he reached them, he handed Merry a small green plant. Evan could see that it was covered with tiny white berries. The crowd watched, clearly awed by this exotic stranger.

The Sheriff, who had been momentarily shocked into silence, struggled to regain control. "Yes, a time for *giving*," he mocked. "Look folks, he's giving her a weed. That's right. That's the kind of Christmas you'd have if you left the Complex—*weeds*. Trees in your *house*. Only one day of gifts!" The Sheriff's face was purple from shouting.

Merry stared from the plant to her father, mystified.

Evan jumped down from the boxes and ran to her side. "It's not a weed," he told her. "It's mistletoe. It's a tradition, remember?"

Merry's face lit up. Standing on her tiptoes, she held the mistletoe over her father's head. "This is what Christmas is about," she said, and then she kissed him sweetly. "The gift of love."

Captain Kringle's face softened, then crumpled as he held out his arms and hugged his daughter tightly. "It's the best gift I could ever hope for," he told her, his face glowing with love and pride.

He straightened up and held his hand out to Evan. "Thank you, son."

The Sheriff began his rant again. "Captain Kringle, you're finished! Turn in your badge." He spun around and faced the crowd. "How many of the rest of you want to be ruined? For a *weed* and a *kiss?*"

People began to slowly turn away.

"Quick, do something," Evan implored, glancing from Kringle to Merry.

"I can't kiss them all," Merry said hopelessly.

The Sheriff stuck the candy cane into the top of his boot and came toward them, rubbing his hands together.

"Wait, don't go!" Merry shouted to the crowd.

She turned to Evan. "When you sang to me, I could feel the spirit of Christmas. Sing to them! Make them feel it, too."

Evan was trembling and his mouth was dry, but he took a deep breath and began to sing.

> *O holy night, the stars are brightly shining*
> *It is the night of our dear Savior's birth.*
> *Long lay the world in sin and error pining*
> *Till he appeared and the soul felt its worth.*
> *A thrill of hope . . .*

Evan heard Merry's voice join his, and the sound of their pure voices filled the Complex. The crowd stopped shifting around and stood still, listening intently. Merry and Evan finished singing and gazed out at the crowd, who stared back. The silence was deafening.

"I think you're on the right track," Kringle said under his breath.

The Sheriff signaled to the Police, who quickly marched

into formation and encircled the small group. But the crowd was pressing forward, clamoring for more music like starving people clamoring for bread.

Ignoring the menacing expressions on the faces of the Police surrounding him, Evan took a deep breath and began to sing again.

> *Said the night wind to the little lamb,*
> *"Do you see what I see?*
> *Way up in the sky little lamb,*
> *Do you see what I see?*
> *A star, a star, dancing in the night*
> *With a tail as big as a kite,*
> *With a tail as big as a kite."*

One by one, other voices joined in. First Merry's, then Noel's. Kringle laid a hand on Evan's shoulder as he added his deep voice to the song. Merry's dad reached for her hand as he sang, a broad smile growing on his face. Their singing grew louder and louder until it buried the Sheriff's strident calls for order.

The whole crowd was singing now, moved by a primeval spirit to sing the words they didn't even know they knew.

Said the king to the people everywhere
"Listen to what I say!
Pray for peace people everywhere.
Listen to what I say!
The Child, the Child, sleeping in the night
He will bring us goodness and light,
He will bring us goodness and light."

The very walls of the Complex shook with the music. Evan could see things falling off shelves in the stores beyond the crowd. And then, to his utter amazement, the walls of the Complex began to crumble and fold gently to the ground. As the walls slipped lower, the people sang louder. They joined hands with their neighbors, and their faces were radiant with a pure joy. The last notes of the song rang out into the cold evening air and echoed up to the cloudless sky overhead. Evan glanced over at Kringle, who was glowing with satisfaction. The crowd was silent, awed. All that remained of the Complex was a ring of rubble.

The Police Navidad stood frozen in their military formation, gazing helplessly at the Sheriff, awaiting an order.

Before the Sheriff could find his voice, Captain Kringle

pulled himself up to his full height and looked the men he commanded straight in the eye. "Now, Dasher and Dancer, Prancer and Vixen, Comet and Cupid and Donner and Blitzen"—the men lined up in front of him and the Captain made a shooing motion with his arms—"Dash away, dash away, dash away all!"

Evan and Merry collapsed in helpless laughter as the Police Navidad ran from the ruins of the Complex, tripping and falling over each other in their haste to escape. The Sheriff stood shifting from foot to foot in rage. He opened his mouth to speak, but Kringle merely held up one finger, then pointed in the direction of the fleeing Police. With a pathetic last attempt at dignity, the Sheriff spun on his heel, only to have the candy cane he'd stuffed into his boot hook around his knee and send him crashing to the ground. Scrambling to his feet, he followed his men in rapid retreat, the roaring laughter of the crowd chasing him down the hill.

As the last of the Police Navidad vanished over the horizon, the crowd grew quiet again. Merry's mother and sisters pushed their way up to the front and wrapped their arms around Merry and her father.

The silence was broken by screams of joy as the children discovered that, while the Complex may have been reduced to

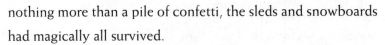

nothing more than a pile of confetti, the sleds and snowboards had magically all survived.

Squealing with delight, they hurled themselves down the hill and away from the Complex. More than a few of the adults joined in, and soon the hillside rang out with shouts and laughter and cries of "Merry Christmas!"

"Well," Evan said, "it looks like there's going to be Christmas after all."

"How are we ever going to get the castle ready for the Christmas feast?" Noel worried.

Kringle smiled at Noel, and resting his hands on the small man's shoulders, turned him to face the castle on the hillside.

Evan turned to look also. "Wow!" he breathed.

The castle was aglow. Banners and streamers fluttered from the ramparts, and torches glowed above the doorways in the growing dark. Evan just knew that smells of cooking and spices filled the enormous kitchens, just as he knew that the perfect tree now stood in the Great Hall, festooned with lights and waiting to be dressed with glittering decorations.

As the townspeople paused in their sledding to gaze at the vision on the hill above, one perfect, bright, shining star appeared in the night sky above the tallest tower of the castle.

"Well, I can't be standing here all night," Kringle declared. "It's Christmas Eve, and I have work to do!"

With Noel trotting by his side, he swept outside with Evan and Merry and the entire Kringle family following in his wake. At the bottom of the hill, the crowd lifted Merry and Evan high on their shoulders, and then the entire village marched toward the castle—toward Christmas.

Eleven

THE GREAT HALL of the castle was humming with the excitement of the Christmas feast. Huge tables draped in linen and damask lined the walls of the room. Giant platters heaped with mouthwatering goodies were being carried up from the kitchens and arranged on the tables. People were climbing ladders to drape evergreen swags from high upon the walls. An-other group was placing gold and silver glass balls on the mag-nificent tree that dominated the center of the room. Children were running around, fueled with excitement and sugarplums. Above the commotion, the music of carols filled the air.

Evan sat at one of the long, cushioned benches that ran alongside the tables, his back leaning against the wall. He wasn't even tempted by the delicious smells from the feast in front of him. Despite the long day and the excitement, or maybe because of it, he just didn't have any appetite.

Merry slid onto the bench next to him. She was wearing a fancy green velvet dress with a big bow, and a wreath of holly held her curls away from her face. Grabbing an orange from the silver bowl on the table, she quickly peeled it and popped a section into her mouth. "Want one?"

Merry glowed with happiness, her face lit with a joy that words couldn't express. Evan noticed that her dress was the same color as her eyes. He also noticed that she was actually very pretty. Suddenly shy, he pretended to be very interested in the goblet of wassail in front of him.

"Well, you did it," he said to Merry. "You brought Christmas back to the castle."

"It wasn't me alone," Merry said earnestly. "I never would have known if it wasn't for you, Evan. You showed me what it could be like. You gave me—my whole family—the gift of the Christmas Spirit."

Evan followed Merry's gaze across the hall to where her dad and mom stood with Kringle. The three adults were laughing and smiling. Merry's dad had his arm around his wife's waist, and Evan watched him drape the other arm around Kringle's shoulders.

"Your dad looks happy to meet his great-great-great . . . you know, his long-lost relative," Evan said.

"He said we could call him Father Kringle, if we wanted," Merry said. "He offered to let us live here in the castle with him."

"Will you?" Evan asked.

"I don't know," she said. "It would be fun to have the spirit of Christmas around all the time, but I think Mom and Dad were a little concerned about Holly and Ivy's plan to start wearing crowns."

Merry looked closely at Evan and frowned. "How come you seem so sad? Wasn't this what you wanted to happen?"

Evan shrugged. He *was* sad. The elation of the victory over the Sheriff, and the heroes' parade, had made him forget the original reason he had wanted to meet the master of the castle. But now, as families settled in next to each other at the big tables, laughing as they passed huge platters of food, parents smiling indulgently as they gave their children seconds and thirds of dessert, Evan felt deeply, desperately homesick.

"It's funny," he said softly. "Everyone got their wish but me."

Just then, Kringle appeared at their table. Evan thought he looked plumper, his robes stretching a bit to cover his belly. As if he could read Evan's mind, Kringle chuckled and patted his stomach. "Plenty of good food here. You should eat up, Evan."

"I'm not so hungry."

"Not losing hope, along with your appetite?" Kringle teased gently.

Evan looked up. "Do you mean . . . ?"

"Of course." Kringle smiled broadly. "I'll take you home tonight. I've got a few stops to make anyway," he said with a wink.

Evan's appetite suddenly returned with a vengeance, and he turned to Merry. "Please pass that figgy pudding!"

THE TORCHES WERE burning down in their holder when Noel found Evan. "Ready to go?" he asked.

Evan looked around the Great Hall. People were gathering up their children, sleepy babies draped over shoulders, younger children following behind, yawning widely. Shouts of "Merry Christmas" and "Good night" rang through the room. Evan looked for Merry, but he didn't see the bright green of her dress anywhere in the crowd. He didn't want to leave without saying good-bye, but at the same time, he felt a kind of relief. He couldn't bear the thought of saying farewell to her face.

"Ready," he said to Noel. And with one last look around the Great Hall, Evan turned and walked outside. He followed Noel around to the back of the castle. "Where are we going?"

"To the stables," Noel replied matter-of-factly.

There was nothing matter-of-fact about the sight that greeted Evan's eyes when he stepped into the cobblestone courtyard of the stables.

A huge red sleigh, with ornate carvings and bright silver runners, sat gleaming in the moonlight. Eight reindeer, their antlers silhouetted against the stone walls of the stable, stood patiently, their tiny hooves resting lightly on the snow-dusted

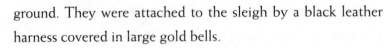

ground. They were attached to the sleigh by a black leather harness covered in large gold bells.

"Can I touch them?" Evan whispered.

"Go ahead."

"Hello," Evan said as he walked up to the reindeer in the lead. The reindeer dipped his head and regarded Evan with patient eyes the color of caramel. As Evan stroked the thick fur fringing the reindeer's neck, Kringle came around the corner of the stables, toting a huge sack. With a grunt, he hoisted the sack up and into the back of the sleigh.

"It'll be a tight squeeze," he said to Evan. "But I think you'll be able to wriggle in right next to Noel."

Noel was scampering around, checking the harness and polishing the sides of the sleigh with a soft cloth. He was fairly vibrating with excitement. "I've never made the trip before," he told Evan.

"I need your help," Kringle said with a smile. "We're behind schedule this year."

Kringle and Noel climbed up into the sleigh, settling themselves among the warm fur blankets piled on the seats. As the reindeer snorted and stamped impatiently, Noel held his hand out to help Evan up into the sleigh.

"Wait! Don't leave!" Merry came running out into the court-yard. She had changed into a long, white flannel nightgown and her long curls tumbled to her shoulders. Evan thought she looked like the Christmas angel.

"Were you going to leave without saying good-bye?"

"I was looking for you, inside," Evan said.

Merry walked over to the sleigh to stand next to Evan. "Well, I guess this is good-bye, then."

Evan just looked at her, his arms hanging awkwardly by his side. "Well, yeah, good-bye," he said, half raising his arms as if to hug her before pulling back, embarrassed.

"For Pete's sake, Evan," he heard Noel mutter.

Merry started to laugh as she stepped closer, and pointed above Evan's head. Evan looked up and saw Noel, a huge smile on his face, dangling a piece of mistletoe over his head.

Merry put her hand on his shoulder and kissed Evan's beet-red check. "Good-bye, Evan," she said. "I'll never forget you."

Evan smiled. "I'll never forget you, either."

Grabbing Noel's outstretched hand, Evan clambered into the sleigh, pulling a fur blanket up to his chin.

"Here we go," Kringle said, and with a sharp whistle to the reindeer, the sleigh began to move silently over the ground.

Evan watched over the curved edge of the sleigh as the castle receded into the distance, until it was just a tiny, golden speck of light. As they flew into the smooth, black sky Evan suddenly felt the air ripple. And then they were out of the snow globe, flying close enough to the stars that Evan felt as if he could reach out and grab one in his hand. The moon, full and pale silver, shone ahead of them.

"First stop: Holidayle," Kringle soon called out over the rush of the wind.

"Can we do a flyover, so Evan can see his neighborhood from the air?" Noel begged.

Kringle nodded, and the sleigh swooped low over the rooftops. It skimmed over the parking lot where the last few unsold Christmas trees rested against Leon's trailer.

Evan hung over the edge of the sleigh, gazing down at his town. His heart was nearly bursting. He was home.

"How cool is this?" Noel leaned over the edge next to Evan and gave him a nudge. Evan had been leaning so far over the side of the sleigh, that Noel's elbow nudged him off balance.

"You can't both lean like that! You'll tip the sleigh!" Kringle shouted urgently.

But it was too late. As the reindeer struggled to hold the

sleigh on course, it dipped just enough to spill Evan over its side.

Evan felt oddly calm as he hurtled through the Christmas Eve sky.

"Don't worry!" he heard Kringle yell out. "You'll be okaaaay." Kringle's voice and the sleigh faded into the distance.

⌒

EVAN CRACKED OPEN his eyes, figuring he had landed in the softest, warmest snowbank ever. He blinked. It seemed awfully bright for nighttime, he thought in confusion.

"Evan, honey, can you hear me?"

Evan opened his eyes fully and looked up into his mother's tearstained face. He was home, in his bed. Every single light in his room was turned on.

"Hey, Mom," he said. "What's wrong?"

His voice was scratchy and when he tried to sit up, he realized he had a crashing headache.

"Take it easy, Ev. Let me help you." His dad appeared at his side, propping up pillows and gently helping Evan to lean back against them.

Evan looked around. Kelly and Elyse stood against the bedroom wall, their faces pale against the bright blue wallpaper.

"Oh, honey." His mother was stroking his hair and crying softly. "We thought we'd lost you."

"Honestly, Mom, I was trying to get home the whole time," Evan protested.

"We know you were," she said. "But when we found you, you were unconscious in the ravine."

"You must have gotten lost in the blizzard," his dad said. "And fallen and hit your head."

"It's a miracle we found you." His mother's voice was choked. "If it hadn't been for your friend Leon . . ."

"Leon?"

"The little man who sells Christmas trees," Elyse said, creeping closer to Evan's bed.

"He's here, sitting in the living room," Kelly said. "He's been really worried about you. Do you want to see him?"

Evan nodded and Kelly slipped out of the room.

"Leon's the one who helped us find you," Evan's dad said. "He said he saw you taking the shortcut through the woods on the night of the storm."

Kelly came back into the room, pulling Leon by the arm.

"Hey, buddy," Leon said, walking up to the bed.

Evan blinked his eyes hard. "Noel?"

His mother laughed. "Sounds like your brain's been mixed up by that knock to your head. This is your friend Leon."

"Quite an adventure you had, huh, buddy?" Leon winked. "You dropped your backpack when you fell; I thought I'd return it." Leon handed Evan's battered orange backpack to him.

Evan fumbled with the zipper. He reached in and pulled out the snow globe.

"Ohhhh," Elyse sighed. "Where did you get that? It's so pretty."

Evan didn't answer. He had his face pressed up against the glass, staring intently at the castle. There! He looked more closely, just to be sure. A small figure dressed in white stood in one of the tower windows. If Evan squinted his eyes just right, he swore he could see the figure waving.

He smiled and gently put the snow globe down next to his bed, then grinned at his mom and dad. "I'm starving," he said.

⌒

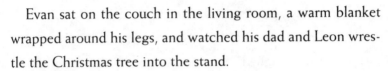

Evan sat on the couch in the living room, a warm blanket wrapped around his legs, and watched his dad and Leon wrestle the Christmas tree into the stand.

"How come the tree wasn't up?" he asked.

"We were so worried about you that we never even got around to getting one," his father said. "Leon brought this one over tonight."

"We weren't going to have Christmas without you," Elyse said staunchly.

"Yeah, Christmas is about family," Kelly said. She didn't even roll her eyes.

Evan's mom came in with steaming mugs of cinnamon hot chocolate topped with towers of whipped cream.

Evan sipped his. "Mmm, good," he said. "But you know, we should have wassail sometime."

His father said, "What the heck is wassail, anyway? Every time I hear that carol, I wonder what they're singing about."

"Funny you should ask, Dad," Evan said.

While Leon and his dad strung the lights on the tree, Evan explained the tradition of wassail to his family. They all agreed it sounded delicious.

Everyone pitched in to decorate the tree, and it was finished in no time. Leon left, after agreeing to come back for Christmas dinner the next day. Evan's mom moved from room to room, turning out the lights until the room was lit only by the glow of the fire and the tiny lights on the tree.

"Time to hang the stockings, then off to bed for all of you," Evan's father announced. He handed the stockings to Evan. "Do you want to do the honors tonight?"

Evan shook his head and handed them to Kelly and his mom. "Let's do it like we always do. It's our family tradition."

His dad sat next to him on the couch and boosted Elyse up into his lap. She rested her head on his chest, her eyes already blinking sleepily.

Evan sighed with happiness as he watched his mom and sister fuss with the stockings, getting them just so: Mom, Dad, Kelly, Evan and Elyse. Then his mom and Kelly came over and sat down on the couch, too, and the whole family listened to the snap and crackle of the fire as it burned down.

It was Evan who began to sing. And as he sang the familiar words of "Silent Night," his heart was full to bursting. It was full of love, full of traditions, and full of the Christmas Spirit. And that night, Evan vowed that he would always keep the traditions alive.

Epilogue

I LEANED BACK in my chair, exhausted. It was the first time I had told the story from beginning to end. The room was silent. The snow had stopped, but night had fallen and all I could see was my reflection in the window. The kids sat motionless in their spots. Had I bored them to death?

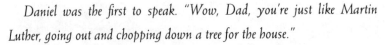

Daniel was the first to speak. "Wow, Dad, you're just like Martin Luther, going out and chopping down a tree for the house."

"We totally have to go out and get one now," Sam added. "If we don't, we're like, breaking a chain that's hundreds of years long."

"Guys, I don't know if you noticed," I said, pointing to the window. "But it's pitch dark now—I don't think we can go tromping around in the woods to get a tree."

"We don't have to go far," Sam protested.

"Yeah, it's nothing compared to what Evan went through," Daniel said.

"And Merry," his sister added.

I looked at Jen, who smiled and shrugged.

"All right," I said. "Grab your gear."

Armed with flashlights and bundled against the cold, we marched to the front door, prepared for an adventure.

I threw the door open and, behind me, heard a collective gasp.

A perfect Christmas tree leaned against our porch. A huge white tag fluttered from a red ribbon tied to its top branches. "TO EVAN DARLING AND FAMILY" it said. "MERRY CHRISTMAS."

"It's the magic of Christmas," Lily breathed.

And standing there with my family, their faces glowing with wonder, I had no doubt that it was.

Well, we dragged the tree into the house and set it up by firelight. Just as we finished, the lights flickered, and then came on. We plugged in the tree lights and hung the stockings and sat together, admiring the way the sparks from the dying fire reflected like little fireworks in the colored glass balls on the tree.

"Time for bed," Jen said at last.

The kids stood up and came over to where I sat on the couch, stuffing the last bits of tissue back into the ornament boxes. They all piled on next to me and Lily wrapped her arms around my neck. I got up to give her a piggyback ride upstairs to bed, and she whispered, "Can you still sing the song, Daddy?"

I nodded, and drawing my family close, began to sing.

As their voices joined mine, I knew that the spirit of Christmas was alive—and that here, in my home, my castle, I was the keeper of the magic of the season.